Happy Reading Alison!

Charmed
Spirits

D1522320

CARRIE ANN RYAN

ISBN: 1623220092
ISBN-13: 978-1-62322-009-9

DEDICATION

To Kelly Mueller. Thank you for being my Pack Beta. You rock chica.

.

ACKNOWLEDGMENTS

This is a new series for me so I always need to talk it out with my crit partner and best friend, Lia Davis. Thanks for loving Jordan. She's the first heroine we had that we both went, 'wow', for. So thank you for being by my side for all of this. Devin, Donna, and Tamara, thanks for reading through and helping Charmed Spirits find a home. I couldn't have done it without you. Thanks Scott, again, for a wonderful cover. And thank you Hubby for supporting me when I said, "Hey, I want to write a romance about a witch. Okay?"

As always, a thank you to my readers. You guys are the reason I get to do this. So thank you. I love hearing from you and really, your letters always perk me up.

Chapter 1

"The road to salvation is found through cleansing your heart and finding the right path. Turn your back on those with wicked ways."

Jordan Cross switched off the radio in her '68 Mustang.

"Really? They're still preaching that garbage? It's 2012 for freak's sake," she mumbled to herself, and drummed her fingers on the steering wheel.

She came up to a sign and rolled her eyes at the message.

"Yeah, sure. *Welcome to Holiday, Montana.* Right. Like that would ever happen. And, Jordan, you really need to quit talking to yourself or they'll think you're crazier than they already do."

On second thought, maybe adding new quirks to her repertoire would enhance her wickedness. She smiled and took a sip of her Coke, her gaze on the empty road ahead of her. She practiced her cackle and looked out on the barren hills and plains of Holiday, Montana.

Okay, so it wasn't barren. She just hated it so much she wanted it to be barren so it would reflect that. Trees reached to the sky, their fall colors reminiscent of a harvest sunset. Deep greens, burnt oranges, and crisp apple reds dotted the tree line. Mountains carved through the skyline, towering over the valleys beneath them. Rivers and streams cut through the rolling meadows and beautiful clearings creating a freaking stunning landscape. Any second now Bambi would frolic through.

She knew she needed to stop the bitter attitude. After all, her life's work—well, the one she hid from peering eyes—depended on nature and all its bounty. Still, that didn't mean she had to like the fact she'd returned to Holiday.

"I'm back."

She rolled her eyes and squinted until she saw the first building. Ah, downtown Holiday. Still as adventurous as ever. With the ten buildings on Main Street, it was a regular old metropolis. She already missed take-out and late-night movies. No matter, she'd only be here for a few weeks. Two months tops. Then she'd drive off like a bat out of hell—again.

Jordan let out a sigh and forced herself not to turn around and step on the gas and run. No, not race away exactly; just strategically not be anywhere near the place that had stolen so much of her life. She'd lived in Holiday for eighteen years, five with her folks before they'd crashed their plane into the side of a mountain, the rest with her grandmother who doted on her with sharp-as-glass type of love.

A pang shocked her heart, and she bit her lip. She couldn't think about that now or the fact that the only reason she was even here was because her grandmother was gone. She'd been overseas at an event for her old employer and hadn't even known her grandmother was sick. In fact, she hadn't spoken with her in years. Not since the last fight that had torn them apart. Jordan hadn't wanted to return to find her legacy, but her grandmother had wanted her by her side. It was only because of a lost phone message that Jordan had even heard that her grandmother had passed away. She'd missed the funeral and all the arrangements. Thankfully, her grandmother's friends, the Coopers, had taken care of everything.

Now Jordan was left to clean an old, abandoned house and sell it in a small town where all the citizens hated her. She blinked back the tears she refused to shed and pulled into a parking spot in front of the general store—not a Walmart in sight. The town looked as though it had a modern tilt meshed with an early twentieth century flair— with the small-town attitude that came with it.

Jordan turned off the car, the dull hum of her engine quieting. People milled past, casting curious looks her way.

They all gave her a look that reflected the same thing: 'Who is that stranger?' A look of recognition soon followed, and a look of contempt replaced curiosity.

Hmph. If they looked beneath the surface, they'd see the girl they'd kicked and poked until she ran. They'd see the girl who'd tried to stand tall but hid behind the brown-haired boy who loved her.

She cursed and got out of the car. Already, the memories of why she'd left assaulted her. How was she supposed to make it through a couple months? She grabbed her purse, slammed the car door, and walked into the General Store.

Old Mr. Clancy stood behind the counter, a smile on his face and a story on his lips. God, some things never changed. When she was young, and when Matt hadn't been around, he'd sneak her bubble gum or Tootsie Pops when the other kids had teased her.

Matt.

She closed her eyes and fought to breathe. He couldn't be on her thoughts; she wouldn't let him. Yes, he still lived here, but for all she knew, he was happily married with his three point five babies and a puppy. He, above all others, deserved that.

Jordan took a deep breath and grabbed a pack of gum and a Coke. She really didn't need anything, but if there was one way to announce her presence, it was to show up at town central and wait for the busybodies to do their jobs—whispering through the grapevine to announce her presence. She could have shown up with a bang, maybe on a broomstick or something, just to live up to her name. But witches didn't fly... Well, at least not in her case.

Jordan Cross might be a witch, but she wasn't a pointy-hat-wearing, card-carrying member of the green-skinned race. Nope, she was just a normal woman with a few extraordinary talents.

Those talents had scared the hell out of the bigoted townsfolk and caused her to run like a frightened little girl. Energy pooled within her, and she inhaled again, calming herself. The last thing she needed was to welcome her townsfolk with a display of magic.

At least not yet.

She'd keep that up her sleeve, just in case.

Jordan perused the aisles, waiting for someone to notice her and, if she were honest with herself, procrastinating about going home—no, her grandmother's home. If just going down Main Street had made the memories so fresh they were like gaping wounds, she couldn't imagine seeing the two-story cabin. People strolled in and out of the store, not paying attention to her.

"Did you hear about last night?" A woman in her mid-fifties who Jordan didn't recognize was talking to Mr. Clancy.

The shop owner nodded, his eyes bright under bushy white eyebrows. "Another sighting."

Jordan's interest perked up, and she dragged her fingers over a bag of M&M's, trying to look nonchalant. A spy she would never be, but she could try.

"This time it was by Betty across the street. She swore she heard chains!"

Mr. Clancy let out a bellow of a laugh. "Really? So, this is Jacob Marley, now?"

The lady sniffed but smiled. "Who knows what Betty saw? But I think something should be done about the old Marlow place. Kids are forever trying to break in and damage things. I know we don't want to tear or burn it down because it's been deemed historical, but it's dilapidated and a menace to this town."

"Ah, now, Mrs. Jacobs, don't think that. That place has history. It just happens to have a ghost."

"But really, we would be much better off without that eyesore, we should just burn the thing down. We have enough historical things around town as it is."

The old man shook his head. "You really need to stop thinking that way. We can't do it."

Jordan started and almost dropped her gum. Had she heard right? A ghost in Holiday? Oh, that was rich. The town that had kicked her out for being a witch wanted to burn down a house because they thought it held a ghost in it.

She shook her head and walked toward Mr. Clancy to check out. She'd seen a few ghosts in her time, but they'd been harmless, just pale shells of their former selves who couldn't let go. Not a reason to tear down a building. Maybe she'd check out the old Marlow place while she was here. It would give her something to do other than bury herself in memories and avoid Matt.

"Jordan?"

Jordan dropped her gum and unopened Coke, the can rolling to the booted foot of the man with the voice that haunted her dreams.

She raised her head, unable to speak, as he picked up the can. He had the same brown hair with honeyed streaks. It was longer now in the front than it had been when they were younger. Perfect for her fingers—no, she couldn't think that. His blue eyes looked even sexier with his aged face, not old, but not an eighteen-year old boy either. No, this was a thirty-year-old man with the hard body to prove it.

She straightened her shoulders and met his dumbfounded gaze head-on. "Matt."

"You're back."

She gave a wry smile, pushing down the urge to throw herself into his arms or run from the crowd that had gathered around them.

"Looks like it."

He held out his hand, and she grabbed her Coke, careful not to let their skin touch. Even after all these years, she didn't think she'd be able to handle that.

"I was sorry to hear about your grandmother," Matt said, his sympathy reflected in his eyes.

She ignored the dull ache gripping her heart. "Thank you. I know she loved you like her own." Damn, why did she have to go and say that?

Now even more memories flooded her. Memories of her and Matt sitting at her grandmother's table, drinking hot cocoa or making cookies, or planting flowers in the flowerbed on a warm spring day.

She wasn't going to make it. Damn.

"Well, isn't this nice?"

And, so it begins.

Jordan turned slightly as Stacey St. James sidled past her and ran a finger down Matt's arm. He looked down at the stacked blonde-haired woman and gave a slow blink then looked right past her like he didn't care, but he didn't move when she linked arms with him.

Bitch.

Great, it was high school all over again.

"Hello, Stacey."

"Oh, Jordan! It *is* you!" Stacey batted her eyelashes, and Jordan wanted to punch her...hard. "I almost didn't recognize you. Why, don't you look...like you've been driving?"

Yep, even after all these years, Jordan wanted to smack-a-bitch. But, apparently, law enforcement frowned upon that, especially when said bitch was the daughter of the most prominent family in town. Well, other than the Coopers, of course, although Matt and his family had always been warm to her.

And now thoughts of just *how* warm Matt had been with her flooded her mind. Her cheeks heated, and she coughed. Enough of that.

"Well, I drove here all the way from Denver, so, yes; I suppose it would look like that."

"How long are you staying?" Matt asked as he extricated himself from Stacey's clutches.

"As long as it takes to clean out the house and sell it." Jordan couldn't stay any longer than that; she wouldn't make it.

Could that be disappointment in his gaze? No, it had been too long. He couldn't possibly care if she came or went. It had been eleven years. Besides, she'd left without a world. He didn't owe her anything beyond this brief encounter, while she owed him everything.

She hated being in debt to anyone.

Mr. Clancy finally took her purchase, and she slid over some cash before the older man had a chance to speak. Good thing since he looked like he'd seen a ghost—*ha, funny.*

"Have you seen the house yet?" Matt asked, his brows furrowed.

She shook her head and took her Coke and gum back with a small smile to Mr. Clancy. "Not yet. I was on my way over there. I just wanted to stop by for a drink." She squared her shoulders and started toward the exit.

"You might find more than you bargained for if you want to get out quick."

Jordan stopped and pivoted toward him. "Why? It should only take a few days to clean it out then slap on some paint, right?"

Matt shook his head and put his thumbs in his belt loops—too sexy. "Your grandmother got real sick at the end, and none of us knew." Sadness washed over his face, and Jordan held back any similar feelings. "It may take more than you anticipated to get it ready."

She let out a sigh and closed her eyes, counting to ten. "Then I'll just have to deal with it, won't I? I'm here for the duration in any case." After all, she'd quit her PR job, a job that she hated, so she could *find* herself. God, how pathetic did that sound?

"Well, if you need anything, I'm here. And I bet my brothers would help out in a second."

Jordan nodded, a smile forming. Damn those helpful, sexy Cooper brothers. "Thanks, if I need anything, I'll holler. But I hope to do most of it on my own."

Matt nodded, a knowing look on his face.

Damn, he could always tell her emotions and he knew she was out of sorts. She hated their connection now. "Of course. Well, I need to head back to work, but it's good to see you, Jor." He reached out then looked like he'd thought better of it.

She bit her tongue to keep herself from saying anything, or worse, touching him.

"Good to see you too, Matt."

Matt turned, stopped suddenly, and turned back. "And I'm an idiot." He grabbed a pen from the counter and jotted something on a piece of scrap paper near the register. "Here's my number. Call if you need anything."

"Thanks." She took it from him and watched him walk away, his muscular legs encased is snug jeans. Yum. She stuffed the number in her back pocket and walked toward the door. "Thanks, Mr. Clancy."

He winked. "Good to see you, Miss Jordan. Stay out of trouble."

She gave a huge grin. "You know me."

"That's why I said it, hon."

Jordan laughed and walked past a fuming Stacey and through the exit. The sun beat down on her though the wind chilled the atmosphere quickly.

"Just so you know, I'm going to marry Matt. So keep your claws out of him."

Jordan stopped at her car and turned, her body aching at the thought of Matt marrying that shrew. "Good luck." What else could she say? *I hope you break a nail and die, you bleach blonde bitch?*

Stacey sniffed. "And you better be on your way out of town as soon as you're done. Because no one wants you here." Jordan held back a flinch, but remembered the look of compassion on Mr. Clancy's face. Maybe not everyone hated her. Maybe. "No one did before, and nothing has changed. So you can get your witchy butt back in that old clunker of yours and leave."

Jordan put her Coke on the hood of her car and forced herself not to retaliate, at least not physically. Oh sure, she could use magic or cast a spell on her, but Stacey wasn't worth stirring up trouble. "I don't know what I ever did to you, Stacey."

"Don't you?" she spat.

"I honestly don't."

"Do my eyes deceive me? Is that Jordan Cross in *my* town?" A too-smooth voice broke the tension between them, and Jordan wanted to vomit.

"Hello, Prescott, your sister was just

welcoming me to the town." She clenched her keys in her fist, ready to escape. God, she didn't want to be here, not with *him*.

"Ah, Stacey is quite the helper, isn't she?" He wrapped an arm around his sister's shoulders and gave a perfectly fake, megawatt smile.

"As always. Well, if that's all, I'm going to go. Thanks for the welcome." She opened her car door and slid inside. A hand caught the doorframe before she could close the door, and Jordan inwardly cursed.

"Now that you're back, just know that I'm the mayor of this town," Prescott sneered. "And we don't need any of *your* kind here. So watch your step, and I'll be sure to watch it as well. You aren't welcome here, Jordan Cross. And if you *cross* me or my town, I'll stick Sheriff Tyler Cooper on your ass so fast you won't be able to hex anyone this time."

Prescott looked up and narrowed his gaze. "Ah, there is our Sheriff now. You're lucky this time."

Jordan bit her tongue. She didn't hex people. It was a moral rule of hers. But damn Prescott and his insults anyway.

"If that's all..." She tugged on her door, and Prescott pulled away, his fake smile back on his face. "Welcome to Holiday, Jordan."

She slammed the door closed, revved her engine, and pulled away. Jesus, what had she been thinking coming back?

Holiday wasn't her home, not anymore. She'd do her job and leave. She had to because, if she didn't, no amount of spells would protect her heart or her sanity.

Chapter 2

Matt Cooper walked into the hardware store in a daze, his body going through the motions while his mind tumbled in an array of memories, anger, and longing.

She's back.

Jordan Cross, his high school love and childhood best friend...back. She'd left without a word, leaving a mess of dashed possibilities and his broken heart in her wake.

But, Jesus, she looked even better than before.

Her green eyes seemed darker, more haunted or sorrowful, than before, like she'd fought more than she'd bargained for and was still losing. Her hair was longer now, very glossy sable locks falling to the middle of her back in careless waves. He'd had loved to run his fingers through it when they sat at the lakeside watching the sun set.

Yes, they'd been that clichéd in high school, but he'd loved her.

Loved.

Past tense. Because he didn't love her anymore. She'd left him. Left him with his problems, his everything and yet nothing.

Matt shook his head and went behind the counter, trying to ignore the dull pain in his temples. *Darn witch, she shouldn't be here.* He didn't want to think about her. Didn't want to deal with it all over when she left again.

But, she'd looked so lonely in that store, even surrounded by people.

Without her grandmother, she *was* alone.

Dammit. He couldn't think like that. She didn't want him. She'd proven that when she'd left. She'd even had the forethought to leave the ring on her pillow for him. He dug his hand in his pocket and gripped the small circle of white gold and the little diamond he'd been able to afford.

Right, so why had he put it back in his drawer that morning instead of returning it? Why had he kept it all this time? And why, for some odd, unknown reason, had he stuck it in his pocket this morning? Maybe Jordan had whispered something on the wind, and he'd heard. She was a witch after all.

"Boss? You okay? You look like you've seen a ghost," Brad, his assistant, asked as he leaned against the counter next to him.

The irony of that statement was not lost on Matt.

He cleared his throat and took the binder off the counter to check inventory. "I'm fine."

"Really?" Brad asked, his eyes wide. "And seeing Jordan Cross didn't do anything to you?"

Matt turned, eyes wide. "How the hell did you find that out so fast? You've been in the store the whole time."

Brad smiled and wiggled his iPhone. "Modern technology and Facebook. There's already a poll going on the Holiday Page to see if the two of you get back together." He leaned closer, grinning. "So, you have any inside scoop?"

Matt snorted. "Unfreaking believable, and even if I did, I wouldn't give it to you." He shoved the binder toward his assistant and shook his head.

"Go do the inventory and tell Sally to man the register. I'm going out for the day."

"To Jordan?"

"Fuck off."

"Hey! Watch your language. I'm your employee, and you could corrupt me."

"Yeah, and I knew you when you were in high school, smoking weed behind the bleachers and trying figure out how to get in Sally's pants. I could always tell Sally about how you feel if that would make us even."

Brad paled and looked frantically over his shoulder. "Exnay on the pants thing. Okay?"

"Just because you failed at your attempt, doesn't mean you didn't try."

Brad let out a sigh. "Tell me about it."

Matt laughed. "I'm going to head over to Jackson's. He wanted me to check out the banister because one of the balusters looked loose. Don't steal from the register."

Brad put his hand over his heart, his eyes wide. "*Moi*? I can't believe you'd think that!"

Matt raised a brow. "Uh huh. *Adios*."

"Say hi to Jordan for me," Brad teased.

"Sure thing. And say hi to Sally."

Brad blushed and cursed under his breath as the cute redhead came up to the register, completely unaware of his decade-long crush.

Unrequited love. A bitch at its finest.

Matt got into his Chevy and started toward Jackson's. His eldest brother still lived in their family home since no one had wanted to sell it after their parents had died in the car accident that haunted the Cooper brothers' dreams. Matt lived in a small apartment above his hardware store, though eventually, he'd planned to move to a home he could build on and make his own. After all, he wanted to raise a family. It was just the whole finding-a-wife thing that got in his way.

He pulled up beside his brother Justin's Jeep and turned off his truck. He hopped out and grinned at his older brother. Well, *all* of his brothers were older, but that was beside the point. Justin was his height at around six foot one but wore his hair slightly shorter. They all shared the same blue Cooper eyes, though.

"Hey, you here for dinner?" Justin asked, a grin on his face. His brother grinned often these days and was pretty laid back, a far cry from the troublemaker he'd been in his youth. Now the elementary school principal could smile and laugh with the best of them.

Matt nodded. "Yeah, I got here early to fix one of the balusters on the railing for the staircase. Why are you here so early? I don't even think Jackson is here yet."

Justin shrugged as he opened the door. "I got off early and didn't want to go home only to have to come back here. I figured I'd start on dinner, drink a beer, and watch the game while I waited for everyone to show up."

Matt laughed and searched through the toolbox that the ever-prepared Jackson had left near the end of the stairs for him.

"What are we having?" he asked as he set to work.

"Chili and cornbread. You want a beer?"

"Sounds good. I'll finish this up. It won't take long, and I'll help you out if you want. Though I do like how Jackson invites us to dinner and we always end up cooking."

Justin shook his head. "Nah, I got it. You know Momma taught us all how to cook. And as for Jackson, he works too much to actually cook. He just likes offering his place because it's bigger."

"Yeah, because she didn't think we'd get married, and she didn't want us to starve." The familiar ache of her loss settled deep in his stomach, though as time had moved on, it didn't burn as deep.

"Well, she wasn't too far off on that, considering we're all still single."

"True." Jordan's face popped in his mind, and he held back a grimace. He really needed to stop thinking about her like that. She might be back now, but she'd leave soon, and he'd be alone. Again. Maybe he should just stick with Stacey.

He held back a shudder. Okay, maybe not.

The front door opened, and another brother, Tyler, walked in, a laid-back smile on his face, a six-pack in one hand and his sheriff's hat in the other. He closed the door behind him and ran a hand over his newly shorn hair.

"I'm surprised you're here this early," Matt commented. "I'd thought you'd have a date."

Tyler grinned full out, his teeth gleaming in the sunlight shining through the windows. "Not tonight, buddy. Like I'd miss dinner with my beloved brothers."

Matt raised a brow. "Got stood up, did you?"

Tyler set the six-pack and hat down on the table in the foyer and shook his head. "It's not my fault my dates talked to each other this morning."

"Dates?" For a ladies' man, Tyler was an idiot sometimes.

His brother shrugged, unrepentant. "I double booked. Sue me."

"You're the law in this town, bro. At some point, you may just have to arrest yourself."

"It wasn't as if I was planning on marrying either of them."

Matt set his tools down and took the offered beer from Tyler. "But you don't have to be an ass about it."

Tyler glared. "I'm not an ass. I'm up-front. I'm not looking for a wife. I don't go out and sleep with every date I have. I'm safe and honest. Just because I messed up my schedule doesn't make me an ass."

Matt smiled, at ease with their old argument. "I give up. You're perfection and I shall bow at your feet."

Tyler scoffed. "It's about time you learned your place. Or maybe go out and find yourself a date." He grinned, and Matt fisted his hands.

He didn't like where this was going.

"I date." Sometimes. Okay, it'd been a few months. Wait, maybe nine? Jesus, he needed to go out. And running from Stacey and her perky...smile...didn't count. Again, Jordan's face came to mind, and he bit back a groan. She'd been in town for only a few hours, and she was already taking over his mind and life. Typical Jordan.

But that was why he'd loved her.

Emphasis on the past tense. Because he didn't love her now. No way.

"You okay in there?" Tyler asked. "Let me guess. This is about a certain brunette high-school sweetheart of yours that came back to town today?"

Matt closed his eyes so he didn't have to see the knowing gaze. No matter what he did, he couldn't avoid her. And, frankly, it was getting harder to tell himself he even wanted to. "I take it you saw the announcement on Facebook?"

Tyler's eyes gleamed. "Oh, I saw the announcement, and the poll on whether you and Ms. Jordan were getting back together."

"Damn, why is it that Holiday loves polls so freaking much?"

"Yep. It's about fifty-fifty right now. But that's because not enough people were there to see the chemistry and don't want to rely on second- and third-hand accounts. So there is another poll on whether or not they should concoct an event to put the two of you together. How does it feel to be a Holiday celebrity?"

Matt fought the urge to punch the smug look off his too-happy brother's face. "I'm a Cooper; I'm already a Holiday celebrity."

CARRIE ANN RYAN

"True. But when the betting gets going, I want to win. So you have any insider's scoop for me?"

Matt threw a small piece of wood at him, and Tyler ducked smoothly. "No, we're not getting back together." *Damn.* "She's just back to clean out her grandma's place then she's leaving." Again.

Tyler nodded, a too-understanding glint in his eyes. "Oh, and just so you know, I saw her today. She's still pretty as ever."

"Watch yourself, Tyler," Matt growled.

"I won't poach. But I will warn you that I had to warn off Prescott already."

Matt went on alert. That fucker. He'd always hated the guy. It was a wonder how he'd become mayor. No, scratch that. No one had wanted the job badly enough to go against the St. James money. "What did he do?"

"Just acted like the ass he was and was a little too close to full-out harassment in my opinion, so I made sure I was around in case it escalated. I couldn't tell if Jordan was relieved or not. You know how she likes to deal with her own problems. But I didn't want her to feel like she was alone as soon as she came back."

"Thanks, Tyler." Though he wished he'd been there to help. But he didn't think Jordan would have welcomed his help.

"No problem, man. You know Jordan was like family back in the day. I hated to see her leave too."

Matt nodded and gave a small smile. "I know."

The front door opened again, and this time, Brayden walked through the door, beer in his hands and grease on his jeans. Fuck, had he missed the BYOB memo? "Shit, Bray, didn't you shower before you came over?" Tyler laughed.

"Shut the fuck up." Brayden scowled, and Matt bit back a laugh. And people said that Bray was the nicest of the Coopers. "I washed up, somewhat. I can't get this stuff off me most days. Deal with it." His black hair curled a bit at the ends and was still wet, proving he'd at least cleaned something.

"Is that Bray?" Justin called from the kitchen.

"Something smells good," Bray yelled back. "Chili?"

"Yep, and cornbread," Matt answered as his stomach rumbled. He took another swig of his beer, the bitter brew doing nothing to cool his thoughts of a certain brunette.

Fuck. He needed to stop thinking about her.

Anytime now.

Justin walked out, drinking a beer. "Dinner won't be ready for a few, but the game's about on."

"Sounds good. The Broncos are going to kick some ass tonight," Tyler said as he walked toward the living room.

The others followed him, bashing the other team and praising their Denver team. The Broncos had been their father's favorite, and the Coopers were loyal to a fault. They sat, drank beer, and watched the kick-off as the smell of chili filled the room.

The front door opened again, and his last brother, Jackson, walked in.

"What the hell?" Jackson scowled. "Just take over my fucking house, why don't you?"

"Hey, at least I fixed the banister for you," Matt retorted. "And Justin cooked for you because that's how we always do things. Stop complaining."

Jackson grunted, went into the kitchen, and came back out with a beer in his hand. He sank into the couch and sighed. It was a freaking Sunday evening and his brother had worked a long hard day because he kept his doors open on weekends to accommodate others in town. He'd taken off his suit jacket and shoes and loosened his tie, but he still looked like a professional. Even if the guy was a dentist. And an ass. But the man was their brother so they couldn't take him out back and shoot him with Tyler's gun. Yet.

Justin's phone beeped, and he ran out of the room, calling, "Chili's been ready," on his way. They grabbed their bowls and ate while watching the game. During the commercials, his brothers teased him about Jordan. Damn. It didn't look like they'd give up any time soon.

Matt checked his watch and cursed. "Okay, I'm out. Let me know how the game ends." The sun was about to set, and he had places to be. Well, one place.

"God, you're a pussy sometimes," Justin teased. "Afraid of the dark, are you?"

"Something like that," Matt said evasively and ran out the door.

He drove his Chevy to his place then hopped out and ran to the old Marlow place, the sun's setting rays beating down on him like a hangman's noose. He barely made it through the door and into the living room when the last tip of the sun went below the horizon. Panting, he looked down at his hands and bit back a sob.

His hands faded to an eerily translucence, his arms, chest, legs, and the rest of him following soon after.

No, he wasn't afraid of the dark or even ghosts.

Because on every full moon...he was one. And it was all Jordan's fault.

Chapter 3

Jordan leaned against the wall, her brain not fully functioning in the early morning heat. It was freaking September in Montana. Why was it so hot? Stupid global warming. She desperately needed a cup of coffee. Damn, she missed the corner shops where she could just walk for a cup of organic brew. Now, she didn't even have a coffee maker, and she didn't want to leave the house to go to the diner to get it because, once she left, she was afraid she'd never come back again.

And this time, she wasn't just talking about the town. Her grandmother's house was scary as hell. When she'd first walked in, she'd almost about-faced and run in the opposite direction. Dust and dirt covered everything that wasn't covered in plastic. Even the plastic looked worn. Cobwebs filled the corners, broken floorboards stood in her way, the doors were off the hinges, and the counters looked like mold had found a new place to live.

Her grandmother had been clean, even as she'd gotten sick. The vandals who had come to take over the creepy house on the corner were not. Jordan would kick every one of their bratty little asses. She'd never thought the house creepy, it was just the fact that her family was a family of witches, so of course the locals thought they were creepy and evil. So freaking close-minded.

They'd ruined her home.

Well, the only home she'd ever known.

"Hey, stranger," a voice called out, and she screamed, her heart racing. "Hey, Jordan! I'm sorry! It's only me."

Jordan turned to see Matt, his face flushed and a small smile on his face.

"Dammit! Stop sneaking around! It's spooky as all hell."

"I'm sorry, Jor."

She ignored the way his nickname for her rolled off his tongue. He shrugged and held out his hands. That's when Jordan noticed the steaming cup of coffee in each hand. Yep, this man was a god. A sexy god. *No. Not thinking that.*

"I figured you might not have a maker, and I remembered how much you love your coffee in the morning."

Damn sensitive, caring, responsible man.

"Thanks," she grumbled, and took a deep gulp, the coffee almost scalding her tongue. At least that would keep her from saying anything stupid like, 'I still love you.' He leaned against the doorway, his blue eyes just as intense as ever, his dark locks begging for her fingers. She tightened the grip on her coffee cup. No, she wouldn't touch. Or even think about touching because that led to things she couldn't run away from.

"So, Matt, why are you here?" *Other than to annoy me.*

"I figured you could use some help. I'm a carpenter after all." He smiled, and it brought a little kick to her chest.

And a carpenter? He could always work with his hands. No. She couldn't think like that, either.

He looked around the house from where he stood and shuddered. "Though, maybe I should have brought a bulldozer."

She fought back a laugh. He was right, but she wouldn't give him the benefit of the doubt. Not when she wanted him out of the house so she didn't have to think about memories better left forgotten.

"I thought you worked at the hardware store." At least that was what a few of the old biddies had told her when she'd picked up her dinner from the diner the night before.

Matt took a sip of his coffee, and she forced herself to not watch the way his throat worked as he swallowed. It was as if she was a teenager again. Though, since the last time she'd seen his blue eyes they'd both been teenagers, she couldn't really blame herself. Much.

"I own the hardware store. But I still do carpentry jobs on the side. I like to work with my hands." He studiously avoided her gaze, and she was grateful.

Damn hormones.

"I'm glad you're doing what you like, Matt." Her voice sounded too whimsical. Damn, she didn't know what she wanted in life and yet the man she had left made her want even more things. Well, maybe not everything. Who could really want Stacey? Matt had changed so much if that was his new type.

"How's Stacey?" She cringed. Had that sounded jealous? Oh, whatever.

"Stacey?" He furrowed his brow then a slow,

wide smile covered his face.

Oh, God. It hurt. Jesus, he loved her.

"Don't tell me you're jealous, Jor."

She raised her chin and fought back the ridiculous notion, on the verge of tears. She would *not* cry over the fact she'd lost her chance when she'd never even had one to begin with.

"Of course not, I'm very happy about your engagement." *Look at that, I didn't throw up when I said it.*

Matt choked on his coffee, his body folding over himself. Jordan rushed to his side and pounded him on the back.

"What...what did you say?" Matt asked once he quit coughing long enough to get some words out.

"I was just saying I was happy you and Stacey are getting married. It's nice to see you moving on." She cringed. That wasn't what she'd meant to say. Now she looked like she was the center of the universe. *Great going, Jordan.*

"Where the hell did you hear that?"

"Uh, from Stacey? Your soon-to-be bride?"

Matt shook his head and looked a bit sick. "Hell, no, Jor. Stacey and I aren't engaged, dating, or even close."

Relief spread through her even as she thought that it didn't matter anyway. She'd leave. But he wasn't with Stacey; she could at least rejoice in that.

"Oh, well, I might have heard wrong." Wait, why was she covering for the blonde bimbo?

Matt shook his head. "Oh, I don't think you did. That woman is a conniving snake."

Jordan threw her head back and laughed with Matt joining her. "Oh, thank God. I was worried it was only me."

"Oh, no. I'm pretty sure the entire town is with you on that front, Jor. Dear God, I wish that woman would move away."

"Or at least shut up."

Jordan drank the last of her coffee, a weight she didn't know she had lifting off her shoulders as she talked with Matt. She'd almost forgotten how close they'd been as friends before they'd dipped their toes in the more serious relationship pools. She could always count on him, though, as it turned out, the same couldn't have been said of her.

"So, you're here to help with carpentry? Well, I'm going to need tons of it." She waved her hands around the room and tried not to wince. "But, I think that may take a backseat for now."

Matt nodded, his gaze roaming over the place with a frown over his face. "I can't believe people would do this." He turned to her, they eyes locking. "I promise you, if me or my brothers had known the extent of the damage, we'd have done something."

She could always count on the Coopers. "But in the store, you hinted." She hadn't wanted to push, but he'd known something.

Matt shook his head. "I'd only guessed the place would be in need of repairs since your grandmother hadn't let anyone in the house for so long. I'd seen it from the outside, so I knew it wasn't good, but I hadn't realized the inside was this bad."

Pain ricocheted through her. Yet another thing that was her fault.

Jordan gave a nod but didn't meet his eyes. How could she?

"Those asses will get what's coming to them, Jor. Don't worry."

She smiled. Yep, that was her Matt. The good guy. Wait, not *her* Matt. Never again, *her* Matt.

"It doesn't matter. I'll get this place cleaned up, sold, and then it won't be an eyesore anymore."

"You mean we."

"Huh?"

"*We'll* get this place cleaned up."

Oh, she didn't know if she could work side-by-side with him for too long. Her already unstable mood swings might go crazier than a menopausal woman in a heat wave. Something she was *not* looking forward to experiencing one bit.

"Why are you helping me?" She had to ask. She'd left him, and yet here he was, being a nice guy.

"Because we're friends." The words looked like they were ripped from him, and she wanted to cry at the situation. "Or at least we were. I'd like to be friends, Jor."

His gaze locked with hers, and she wanted to throw her arms around him or cry. Since she was stronger than that, she did neither.

"I'd like that too." She was proud of how steady her voice sounded when inside she was a wreck of emotions and memories.

Matt smiled and walked farther inside the house. "Okay, where do we start?"

"Start?" How about kissing? That seemed like a good start...No!

He raised a brow and gave her a knowing look. *Jerk.* "In your house?"

"Oh, right. Sorry, the coffee hasn't kicked in yet." She looked at the mess surrounding them and held back a cringe. "I think we need to work on at least cleaning up a bit first then fixing what we need to."

Matt nodded, his gaze studying the room as she tried to pull hers from his jawline. Yum.

"Okay, then. I heard from Mrs. Chambers that you already bought some cleaning supplies at the general store." He grinned, and she shook her head.

"Damn small town."

"Come on, you missed us some."

"Not even a little." She shook her head as he laughed. No, she hadn't missed the town. She missed Matt and his brothers and maybe a few others, but not the town. The busybodies and sharp-tongued residents were the reason she'd left in the first place. Well, at least most of the reason.

Matt held his hand over his heart and staggered back. "I'm hurt."

"Shut it. I don't have time for your pains." Though to soothe them... Geez, this was going to be even harder than she'd thought.

"I like it when you're feisty."

She leveled a look at him and walked toward

the mound of cleaning supplies and trash bags she'd bought the day before.

"That's enough of that. We said we wanted to be friends for as long as I'm here, and you talking like that isn't helping anything." She had to get it out there because, if he kept being his normal charming self, she wouldn't make it.

Matt put down the box of trash bags he held and crossed his arms over his chest. "Okay, there are a few things wrong with that statement. First off, yes, I want to be your friend. We were best friends once, and I'd like to have you back. Second, what the hell is with that 'as long as I'm here' crap? If you leave this time—"

"Not if, when."

He rolled his eyes. "Fine, *when* you leave this time, you don't get to do it without a goodbye and a phone number. We're going to talk once you leave and do what friends do—connect."

Guilt ate at her from the memory of her leaving before, but she buried it. It had been a long time ago.

"And third, I'm being myself with you, Jor. I'm not groping you or kissing you like I'd do if we were more than friends. I was teasing and playing around. That's what friends do. I know this is awkward, and we're not talking about the elephant the size of Montana in the room, but we're going to get through this."

"I don't think it's possible for an elephant the size of Montana to actually fit in this room."

He let out a breath. "It could, and it will, considering our history. Awkwardness doesn't follow the rules of physics; it's one of the commandments or something."

She raised a brow. "Really? God said 'Thou shalt not follow the rules of physics when awkward'?"

"Something like that."

They broke out in laugher, and just like that, the tension eased a bit. They picked up the cleaning supplies and started to work as a team. With each trash bag of junk collected, they reminisced about the times they'd spent in her grandmother's house. She had thought she'd have felt sad in the place where she'd grown up and ultimately rejected, sitting with the man she'd left, but with Matt's smile and laughter, she couldn't quite feel too depressed. As always, Matt made her feel whole again.

Too bad she was going to leave him again once she figured out what she was going to do with her life.

"Do you still practice?" Matt asked as they sat on her porch and gulped down the ice water she had in her cooler.

"Practice what?"

"Witchcraft."

She froze, surprised he'd broach the taboo subject with such ease. "Sometimes."

"Sometimes? That's it? What does that mean?" He took a long drink then leveled his gaze at her.

She shrugged, not comfortable with the topic. He'd always been her protector when she wasn't protecting herself. But he hadn't been there for all if it and hadn't seen what had happened when others found out about her talent. If she could even call it that.

"Jordan?"

With him sitting there with that honest look on his face, she couldn't hold back. He made her feel transparent, so she told him the truth. "I don't practice as much as I'd like. But I'm always using my powers. I mean I can't *not* be a witch. It runs through me; it's in my blood. I just don't do everything that I want to with it."

He rested his hand on hers, and she gripped it tightly, his warmth seeping into her bones. "What do you want to do with it?"

"Like working with potions again or trying

out new spells. Anything, really."

"Why don't you?"

"I don't know." No, that was a lie. She *did* know. But she'd been hiding from herself for so long it was hard to find who she was.

He nodded, but she could tell he didn't believe her. It was just one more reason she liked him; he let her be when she wanted it.

"I hope you have the proper permits for this monstrosity," Prescott said from the edge of the walkway, startling her.

She and Matt stood quickly, her stomach heaving at the thought of having to be in the same space as Prescott. And, oh God, what if he told Matt about what had happened that night?

Matt crossed his arms in front of his chest and shifted so he blocked her from view. She took a deep breath and moved closer to his side. She was a freaking adult. She could handle this. Maybe.

"Jordan owns the place, Mr. Mayor," he growled. "It's not a public place, so she doesn't need a permit to clean it up."

"We'll see." Prescott lifted his head so far Jordan thought she could see directly up his nose and walked away, anger in his stride.

As soon as his car sped away, Jordan

relaxed, they'd been too into each other even to notice him pull up in the first place. She needed to hurry up and get the house sold so she could leave. She might be a strong woman in some respects, but Prescott made her want to crawl in a hole and hide. That, by far, wasn't his worse offense. She hated being weak, but for some reason, she couldn't grow a backbone around him.

"I hate that guy," Matt grumbled.

Jordan gave a small smile. "Me, too."

"Hey, you two, I hear you could use some help." Justin, Matt's very cute brother, walked toward them.

"I think I got it, Justin," Matt growled, and Jordan raised a brow.

Interesting. Was Matt jealous of his big brother? Should she even care that he was? After all, they weren't together, and Jordan thought of the Coopers like her family, just a very sexy one. Matt was the only one who had ever made her want to dream of more. Not in terms of success, but to have him *be* her family.

"I could use all the help I can get, actually." She wouldn't have to be alone in a room with Matt and her traitorous thoughts, and she'd get out of here quicker. That's what she wanted after all, right?

"Sounds good to me," Justin said. "Where do you want me?" He wiggled his brows, and she laughed while Matt growled again.

"You want to take the bathrooms?" she teased.

His face fell. "Seriously?"

"Hey, you're late; it seems only fair." She looked over at Matt and winked.

"Late? You didn't even know I was coming!"

She shrugged. "Not my problem. So what do you say?"

He let out a breath, and Jordan bit back her laughter.

"Fine, whatever." He stomped inside, and she and Matt broke down.

Tears slid down her cheeks and her side ached, but that moment was one of the best she'd had in forever. It was all because of the Coopers. How on earth was she supposed to leave again?

Chapter 4

Jordan closed her eyes and focused inward, her body swaying back and forth in rhythm with the wind music she'd put on her iPod. She sat cross-legged on her grandmother's living room floor; she couldn't think of it as her place. It'd been a month since she'd been in town, and yet, it still didn't feel like home, though Matt and his brothers helped.

They were making it that much harder for her to leave again; that seemed to be their goal. If she were honest with herself, she didn't mind as much as she should.

She shook her head. Damn, she needed to

stop thinking about the Coopers, more specifically Matt. They drove her to distraction, and she needed to focus on her meditation. She took a deep breath, her body slowly returning to that slow motion that ebbed with the minuscule vibrations of the earth.

This is why she loved being a witch. She didn't dance naked in the moonlight—though she remembered that Matt has always wanted her to try it. She didn't paint her face green and cackle at passing schoolchildren—even though it was tempting. No, she was a witch in the true sense of the word. She belonged to Mother Nature, and she could feel the connection to her surroundings sprouting like youngling seeds waiting for the sun.

She stretched her arms above her head, her palms cupped, bringing the energy to her. It wrapped itself around her arms, trailing down her body like tendrils of light. She hummed as the intensity of the light soaked into her skin and dissolved.

Yes, this was why she loved being a witch.

Peace.

She lowered her arms, took a deep breath, and opened her eyes. God, that felt better. She rolled her shoulders and stood in one fluid motion. She'd needed that. The tension in the past month had depleted her resources. Though some people opened their arms to her, some people in town had welcomed her with cool smiles while others openly turned their backs on her. Though she shouldn't have expected anything else. These were the same people who had ridiculed her as a small child and had sided with the enemy...

She shook her head. It wasn't time to think about that. In fact, it was *never* time to think about that.

It wasn't all that bad. She had the Coopers, though she really only saw Tyler, Justin, and Matt. Bray was always busy in the mechanic shop, which he owned, since it was the only one around for five counties and also serviced the ranching and farming equipment. And Jackson... Well, Jackson was Jackson, distant, cool, and a little—no, a lot—intimidating. But he'd held her close when she'd seen him on the street and whispered welcome back before he'd walked away as if it hadn't happened. He'd been the big brother she'd always wished she'd had.

Oh, and there was Abigail, a new friend that she'd clung to. She'd babysat the woman in high school and now she was a stunning, if not alarmingly shy, twenty-two-year-old school teacher. Jordan had always liked her, though they were too different in age when they were younger to really hang out. Now, that seven-year age gap wasn't so much of a problem, and Abby seemed to have adopted her.

Jordan laughed to herself as she walked to

her makeshift office. The little, curvy woman was a force to be reckoned with, though no one realized it behind her quiet demeanor. Well, quiet to everyone else. As soon as Abby lost her shield, she was a little chatterbox, and Jordan loved her to death.

Jordan sank into her grandmother's leather chair, which had survived the vandalism, and unlocked the bottom desk drawer with a key that had been around her neck since she could remember. She lifted the ancient book from its hiding place and set it carefully on the desk before returning the key to her necklace. Each family member wore a similar necklace, though now she was the last Cross. No matter how many keys though, there was just one book.

Her magic book.

Magic floated off the cover in an array of colored swirls and sparkles. She knew no one else could see the colors unless they were magically inclined, though she didn't quite know what else was out there. For all she knew, she was the only true witch out there. Except for the occasional ghost, she'd never seen anything else. That didn't mean they didn't exist though. Jordan always hoped they did. It would be nice to not be so alone.

She shook her head at her melancholy thoughts. This was not the time for that. Her family's magic book, seeping with generations of knowledge and power, sat before her. She should be happy for freak's sake.

Every night, after Matt, and sometimes Justin and Tyler, left for the day, she'd tidy up and come to the office to read the texts. She'd left the book here when she'd run from town. She knew the only reason it hadn't been damaged or stolen while she'd been gone was because of magic. But now it was hers in truth. Her grandmother had been a witch but only possessed a small amount of magic that she used in herbs or to heal the occasional cut and scrape on her and Matt. He'd always been fascinated with it...and so had she.

She hadn't tried any of the spells, and she wasn't sure she was going to. The last time she had...well, it hadn't turned out well.

A knock on the door saved her from having to relive the memoires that she'd worked so hard on burying deep down. She quickly locked up the book and went to the door.

Abby stood on the other side, a hesitant smile on her face, as if she wasn't quite sure of her welcome.

"Hey, hon!" Jor waved her friend in and smiled. She was doing her best to instill some confidence in the smaller woman, but sometimes it was as if she was trying for nothing.

"Hi, Jordan," Abby said, her long brown hair down behind her shoulders and flowing in the wind. Abby was around half a foot shorter than Jordan's five-nine but a few pounds heavier. It wasn't as though she were overweight; it was just that having breasts and hips such as hers tended to distribute differently on such a small frame. To Jordan, Abby's full curves looked pin-up worthy, but to Abby—and others—she looked heavy, unattractive, and stuffed in her clothes. The witch in her wanted to kick some ass on that one, but she didn't know if it would do any good.

"Can I get you anything to drink?"

Abby shook her head and wrung her hands. "No, I'm okay. Well, actually, I came here to see if you wanted to get lunch." She smiled, and Jordan wanted to weep at the beauty.

Really, how stupid were the people in this town? This woman was gorgeous, but Jordan was pretty sure Abby had never been on a date in her life. Asshats.

"I'm starving so that sounds great. But first I need to do some work on the house."

"Oh, okay, I can help if you want."

"Really?"

Abby shrugged then tugged on her lip. "Sure, I don't mind."

Jordan pulled the other woman into the room, and once Abby was out of her jacket, they got

51

to work on the walls. They had to steam off the old wallpaper, and then scrape whatever wouldn't come off right away. She couldn't wait to put a fresh coat of paint on the walls to see what it looked like.

Though she couldn't wait to leave when she had first arrived, she had been drawn back to Holiday. People like the Coopers, Abby, and Mr. Clancy made her feel like the town wasn't that bad. Abby had met up with her at the general store one day and hugged her in welcome, they'd been attached ever since. Maybe everything wasn't as bad as she thought. Then Stacey and Prescott's face came back, filling her vision and she shuddered. Maybe not.

After another hour of hard work, Jordan stood back. "Okay, you ready to eat?"

Abby bit her lip, and Jordan took mercy on the poor woman and grabbed her coat. The October air had cooled dramatically in the past week or so. Halloween was just around the corner and it looked like it would be a cool one this year.

They chatted about their days as they walked to the diner, the air taking on a biting chill as they got closer. They could have driven, but it was a close enough walk that she didn't want to deal with it. Plus, she didn't like leaving her Mustang out on the street where anyone could see it. She didn't trust most people not to do something to her baby when she was away from it.

The diner wasn't too crowded when they got through the door, so she directed Abby to a booth in the corner where they could hide if needed. Even though it grated on her that she even had to think about that crap, she'd rather not make a scene. Again.

They took off their coats and sank into the bench cushions.

"So, what do you feel like eating today?" Abby asked.

"Anything edible, but nothing cold."

Abby laughed. "I thought you lived in New York. It's cold back East too, isn't it?"

"Yeah, but not like this and not in freaking October. I swear the wind is leaching all the energy from my bones every time it blows."

"Weakling," Abby teased in a rare moment of gumption.

Jordan mock-scowled. "You'll pay for that remark."

"Ooh, I'm so scared."

"You should be."

"You wouldn't hurt a fly, Jordan Cross. I don't care what people say; you're a good person." Abby leveled her gaze and lowered her voice. "I know you're a witch, and I'm okay with it. Be yourself. Someone should."

Jordan fought off tears and gripped Abby's hand. "Thank you."

"I like you; it's not hard to."

"Tell that to everyone else."

"I would if they'd listen. But most people don't seem to know I'm alive."

"Then stuff 'em."

"Good attitude."

Jordan's seat faced the door so she could see precisely the moment when Stacey St. James walked through the door on the arm of...Matt.

She shouldn't be feeling the stabbing pain in her chest as it scraped its razor sharp claws around her heart. She bit her lip and blinked rapidly.

"Jordan? What is it?" Abby turned in her seat, and her shoulders lowered. "Oh. You know they aren't together, right? Stacey's tried for so long, but Matt won't hear of it. I don't know why he's here with her this afternoon, but it's not what you think."

"It's not my business what Matt and Stacey do," she whispered, though she'd tried to sound steady and firm.

"It should be."

"Drop it, Abby."

Abby tiled her head and gave a Jordan a look that bordered too much on the side of pity for her taste. "Okay."

"So, like I was telling Matt, it really all depends on the dress." Stacey's voice carried over the small diner, and Jordan resisted the urge to pick up her fork and stab the bitch. Matt had locked his jaw and was trying to extricate himself from her evil clutches. Good man.

Allison, the harried waitress, nodded. "That's great. Do you two want a table? You can seat yourselves." With that, she hurried over to Jordan and Abby's table. When she gave an eye roll once out of Stacey's sight, Allison cemented herself as one of Jordan's new favorite people.

"Hey, guys, sorry it took me so long to get over here," Ally said as she held her hand on her hip and tried not to smile.

"It's okay; I know sometimes it takes a while to get through....people," Jordan teased, and Ally's eyes danced.

"You have no idea." Ally laughed, her auburn hair slowly falling out of its wayward bun.

"How are your kids, Ally?" Abby asked, and Ally's smile brightened and her vivid green eyes sparkled.

"Oh, they're amazing. Aiden is getting so big. I think he's taller than me now, and he's twelve! And Cameron is getting ready for a Halloween play at school. He gets to be the Grim Reaper, so he's excited because he gets to wear the hood. That way he thinks no one will see him if he messes up. And Lacy is loud as ever, but she's my baby." Ally laughed than shook her head. "Look at me go on. Sorry about that. I just love my babies and talk about them as much as I can."

Jordan had met Ally while volunteering at the school to help with the art department. Jordan had been bored and wanted to make sure she gave back and did something with the community. It made no sense just to sit around and let people look down on her, she was stronger than that. The others in town still looked at her like she was a witch and below them, but gradually, maybe she could change that. If not, she had to get over how people thought of her.

Ally was a widow who had lost her husband a couple of years before and had fallen on hard times. She'd done everything she could for her children, but sometimes it didn't seem like enough. Jordan was happy to see her new friend smiling since it was such a rare occurrence when she wasn't around her children.

"I love hearing about them so keep talking,"

Jordan said honestly. That little pang in her heart that she wasn't a mother beat louder whenever she was near Ally, but she ignored it.

"Oh, I could go on for hours, but I still have a job to do." She tilted her head toward Stacey, and Jordan suppressed a groan.

"Okay then, I'll have the club with baked chips on the side and a Diet Coke," Jordan said.

"And I'll have the chef salad with the vinaigrette on the side," Abby said. "Oh, and a water with lemon."

Ally nodded but didn't write the orders down. Jordan suspected she didn't need to as a mother of three. She could remember more than most. "Okay, I'll put that right in." She hurried off, deftly avoiding the bleached bimbo from hell.

"A salad?" Jordan asked. "I thought you said you'd try a burger next time." Jordan wanted her friend to be happy and not worry about her weight.

Abby shrugged. "I'm fine."

Jordan's eyes shot daggers toward Stacey, or at least that's what she wanted. If that bitch hadn't been there, there wouldn't have been a problem. Stacey was always harping on Abby over some small infraction considering a perceived weight problem.

Stupid blonde bitch.

Okay, maybe she needed to tone down on the name-calling. Karma, and all that crap.

"Is there a space for me?" Matt asked as he walked up to their table.

Jordan raised a brow and ignored the rapid beat of her heart at his presence. "I thought you were here with Stacey." She inwardly winced. *God, petty much?*

Matt shuddered then sat in the booth next to her, his body warming her side with an electric current. *Down, libido.* "God, no. She cornered me when I got out of the Chevy. I saw you two walking in here and thought I'd join you, if you don't mind."

"Well—" She didn't want to be near Matt because every time she was, she started to want something more.

Abby cut her off. "We'd love to have you."

Jordan glared, and Abby gave her an innocent look. *Yeah, right.*

"That's good since I told Allison that she could bring my lunch here. Talk about awkward if you'd have said no."

"Matt, your whole life is awkward," Jordan grumbled, but smiled as he kicked her foot playfully under the table.

"True, but that's why I'm glad I have you

two to make me feel better."

Jordan rolled her eyes. "Yes, of course. It's our reason for existence, you know. I mean, if you felt poorly, what on earth would we do?"

They broke into laughter as Ally brought their lunches and drinks.

"Sorry again that it took me so long," Ally said as she set down their food. "I swear, sometimes I just want to... And I should stop right there if I want to keep my job."

Matt leaned over his beef stew and winked. "I won't tell if you won't."

"You are a dork, Matt Cooper. And be sure to tell your brother, Brayden, to stop leaving so much of a tip, will you? People will start to talk."

Matt shook his head. "Hey, he likes the coffee."

"Enough that he comes in every day?"

"Something like that."

Ally rolled her eyes and walked off to help another table.

"You think she knows Bray is in love with her?" Jordan asked.

"How did you figure that out?" Matt asked,

his brows raised.

"It's easy to tell with the way he looks at her." She'd seen it every morning she came in for coffee when she wanted to talk to Ally and get to know her more.

"I wouldn't go that far," Matt answered. "But no, she has no idea. It's kind of fun to watch."

Jordan let out a breath. "Men."

Abby shook her head. "Men."

"Hey, *man* right here."

"You're not a man; you're our friend," Abby teased.

"Ouch, kitten has claws." Matt laughed.

"Meow," Abby said with a completely straight face that had the three of them rolling with laughter.

"You see why I joined your table? You two are great company," Matt said after they caught their breath.

"Thanks," Jordan said dryly. "I'm so glad you think that." She felt all gooey inside at the feel of his body next to her, even with Stacey sitting at the counter, glaring at the three of them. She resisted the urge to wave at the bimbo, barely.

"Any time," Matt said. "As for Stacey, you know I don't beat women, so there is only so much I can do."

Jordan blinked at that statement then burst out laughing again. God, she loved him.

No, bad thoughts, Jordan, bad thoughts.

"Oh, Abby, I forgot. Tyler wants you to call him when you had a chance," Matt said.

Abby paled and dropped her fork. "Wh-why?"

Matt tilted his head, and Jordan furrowed her brows. What was with that reaction?

"He had a question about the upcoming Halloween play and security and thought you'd know the answer."

"Why is there security at an elementary school play?" Jordan asked.

"Because Tyler is paranoid and wants to make sure the kids are okay. Since Justin is the principal, he allows it."

"Then why didn't he just call her himself?" Jordan asked.

"Because he doesn't remember my number," Abby whispered, her head low.

What the hell? "Isn't it in the directory?" she asked.

"Yes, but he never remembers to look there," Abby mumbled. "It's okay; I know what he's going to ask anyway, so tell him that I took care of it, okay?" She looked at Jordan and Matt. "I'm in charge of setting the play up since I'm one of the only teachers who doesn't mind staying late these days."

Matt nodded, a frown on his face.

What was going on?

"I should go take care of that now, then." Her friend put some money on the table and stood stiffly. "I'll see you both later, okay?" She didn't wait for them to say anything back and left the diner in a hurry.

"Okay, what just happened?"

Matt shook his head. "I have no idea, but I think Tyler fucked up."

"If he hurt her..."

"No, I don't think he did it on purpose. In fact, I think he doesn't realize how amazing Abby really is."

A small kernel of jealousy took root, which was ridiculous.

"So he's just an ass?"

"He dates. It's not an issue, but I don't think he's dated Abby."

"Oh...*oh*."

"Right."

"Huh, well, then." Poor Abby.

"The place will be taken down soon. Don't worry," Prescott St. James bellowed over the quiet conversations of the diner. Stacey wrapped her arms around him and hugged tightly. Jordan almost gagged.

"What?" Ally asked, her eyes wide. "You can't destroy the old Marlow place; it's history."

Matt froze beside her, his face going pale.

"Matt?" she asked, worried.

"I can do whatever I need to get done. That place and the old Cross place need to be taken down."

"Excuse me?" Jordan asked, and pushed Matt out of the booth so she could stand. "You can't destroy my home."

"Ah, Ms. Cross. I'm glad you're here, as this will make it easier. Your home is ruining the property values around town. I am making it my personal mission to see that both it and the old Marlow place are destroyed."

"You can't do that." Rage filled her, and she stepped forward to slap the bastard, but Matt held her back.

"She's right, Prescott," Matt stated, his voice a little too shaky for Jordan's comfort. *What is going on with him?* "You can't take down a building because you have a grudge."

Prescott lifted his nose as Stacey gave a trilling laugh that sounded like cats on a chalkboard. "Oh, I can do anything I please. And I will."

"You'll need the council's vote," Matt warned.

"And I'll get it."

"We'll see," Matt and Jordan said at the same time.

"Let's get out of here, Jor. I've suddenly lost my appetite." Matt gave Ally a couple of twenties, far too much for their lunch, grabbed their coats, and dragged her out of there.

Lucky for Prescott because Jordan's magic wanted to kick some ass.

"I don't feel like driving right now. Do you mind if we walk?" He still held her hand, and she clasped it tightly, not wanted to let go.

"Whatever you want."

"Don't say anything you don't mean, Jor."

"What do you mean by that?"

He shook his head. "Never mind."

They walked in the cool sunlight as the wind danced around them. He let go of her hand, only to wrap an arm around her back and bring her closer. She burrowed into his side, grateful for his warmth.

They walked in silence until they ended up by the lake, its water churning in the cool breeze.

"Are you okay, Matt?"

He nodded, but she didn't believe him.

"They won't take your home, Jor."

"I know. But I also won't have any say once I sell it."

Matt didn't answer.

"I *am* selling, Matt. I'm leaving."

"I know." He turned her in his arms, his hands running smooth strokes up and down her back, making her want to purr. "I know." He lowered his head, his lips barely brushing hers in a question.

She closed her eyes and moved the fraction of an inch closer to answer. He tasted of stew, home, and Matt, that heady taste she'd thought long forgotten. He licked the seam of her lips, and they parted. His tongue danced with hers as their grips tightened. She rocked against him, wanting.

He pulled away, leaning his forehead against hers. "I know."

She closed her eyes, lost in the sensation of his touch and the fact that it had no future. Oh God, she didn't want to leave. She wanted to be selfish and stay with him. She wanted to watch Abby bloom and be happy, and she wanted to grow closer to Matt and be a Cooper....but she had to leave. It wasn't her choice, but it had to be done—for the both of them.

Chapter 5

Matt rubbed his palms on his jeans and tried to slow his heart rate. It wasn't as if this was his and Jordan's first date. No, they'd dated plenty of times in the past. That was the thing though. The past. They weren't teenagers anymore running on hormones and sneaking around after curfew.

He didn't know this Jordan, the independent city girl with the grace of confidence. He could still see, though, where she frayed at the edges, particularly whenever Stacey or Prescott happened to be in her presence. He wanted to know more about her. Her hopes, dreams, fears...everything. Right now, it felt as though he were basing his attraction solely on memories. Though he'd had almost a month to get past her defenses, it was only the beginning.

And Jor didn't know anything about him. Not really. She knew the surface, what other people knew, but he wanted her to know more. He didn't know if she could deal with what he turned into every month...and in two nights, he'd have to lie.

He hated lying

Sadly, though, he was becoming very good at it. Just ask his brothers.

Matt sat in his Chevy outside Jordan's home and tried to put on that smooth confidence that so many said he possessed. It sure didn't feel like he had any at the moment. When she'd come back to town, he'd promised himself he wouldn't fall for her again...*as if he'd ever lost those feelings.*

When Prescott had said the afternoon before that he was going to tear down the old Marlow place, Matt thought he'd died on the spot...again. If he really was dead; he wasn't quite sure on that point.

What was he going to do if they tore down the place? If he wasn't in that house at sunset on the evening of the full moon, and the four nights surrounding it, he thought he might be lost forever. Without the house...he might not be found.

And didn't he sound like a pansy? God, something was definitely wrong with him. They were just going on a date. A date that could lead to sweaty, good things if he had anything to say about it.

God...that kiss. He hadn't planned on it. He'd been so wrapped up in his emotions that Jordan's warm little body next to him had made him want more...more than just whatever time she'd give him. He'd placed his mouth against hers but couldn't move the last fraction of space. Thankfully, she'd kissed him back.

So warm.

Wet.

Matt shook his head. It wouldn't be good to show up with an erection at her doorstep. She might take one look down and slam the door in his face. Or worse, find a potion in her spell book to make it fall off or turn green or something. He'd had enough of her potions for a lifetime. He might have loved her once, if not still, but he couldn't be part of her magic. It had destroyed his life. He could watch her from afar and appreciate it, knowing it was a deep and integral part of her, but he couldn't be part of it.

Not again.

Matt got out of the Chevy, adjusted his dick so the zipper didn't dig in quite as much, and started to her door. He clenched his fists and shook his head. Why the hell was he so nervous? He was acting like a fucking teenager.

As he raised his fist to knock, the door swung open, and he almost choked. Dear. God. She was breathtaking. She wore dark jeans that made her long legs look edible, legs that would look even better wrapped around his waist. He moved so his cock wouldn't have a zipper tattoo. Her black boots went up to her knees, but she didn't have those spiky heels that she sometimes wore. Good, because he didn't want her to fall on the almost icy sidewalks. She wore a bright red top with that swoop neck thing that made him want to lick the curve and down to the valley of her breasts. She'd put on a leather jacket, and Matt wanted to take her against the wall.

Hard.

His cock sliding into her pussy, her nails digging into his back...

"Matt? Are you okay? You just groaned." Jordan placed her hand on his arm, and he swore he saw sparks.

He swallowed and nodded. "I'm great. You just look fucking amazing." *Smooth, Romeo.*

She blushed and kissed him softly on the mouth. He wrapped his arms around her so his hands settled in the small of her back and pulled her closer. He didn't deepen the kiss—he didn't want to rush her—but he did lengthen it. God...her taste. Like sweet berries and lilac. He could drown in it and be a happy man.

She moaned, and he pulled back.

"Wow," she whispered.

He kissed her nose and smiled. "That's exactly what I was thinking."

She looked up at him, her hazel eyes imploring. "Should we be doing this?"

"Yes." He didn't hesitate. It might—no, would—end horribly when she left and he had to watch her go. But he wanted whatever time they had.

"Okay." She smiled, kissed him on the cheek, and led the way to his truck.

They piled in and sat for a second. "So, I suck at this apparently. Where do you want to go?"

She laughed, and he joined her. "You didn't plan our first date?" She batted her eyelashes, and he ran his thumb down her jaw. He loved it when her breath caught, and her pupils widened. So responsive, his Jordan.

When he could speak, he cleared his throat. "This is Holiday, Jordan. I could take you down to the lake so we could neck or we can go to my place.

The movie theater doesn't play its movie until Friday, so you're stuck with my boring plans."

She shook her head, her long sable locks falling around her face. He tucked a strand behind her ear, so soft.

"I keep forgetting how small this town is."

"It's not your big city, that's for sure."

She gave him a wry look. "Don't go playing lonesome cowboy with me, Matt Cooper. I know all your tricks."

He held up his hands in mock surrender. "That wasn't a line, darlin'." *Much.* "Why don't you pick the place? I've been everywhere a hundred times."

"How about we grab a bite at the diner and see where it goes from there?"

"The diner? Where we ate yesterday?"

"Is there anywhere else to eat around here?"

He shook his head. "Not unless I cook for you. Which I just might do later on if you'd like."

She gave him a warm smile. "That sounds awesome. Too bad we didn't think of it before hand."

"I had to work all day as it was. That's why I

didn't come help work on the house." He put the truck in gear and drove down the road to the diner.

"It's fine. You don't have to help every day. It's already looking completely re-vamped as it is." She looked out the window, so he couldn't see her face. "It won't be long now."

He gripped the steering well as he heard what went unsaid. *And I'll be gone.* Damn. He was setting himself up for heartbreak, but he didn't much care. He needed her.

He parked, and they got out, the wind biting into his skin as he lifted the collar of his coat. Jordan hadn't waited for him to help her out of the truck, but she did come around and grip his hand.

Ah, marking her territory. He liked it.

He pulled her closer, and they entered the diner. Ally waved and went through the door in the back. He followed Jordan to the back corner booth and slid in beside her.

She raised a brow. "You aren't going to sit on the other side? Doesn't it look weird?"

He shrugged. "So? I want to sit next to my woman."

"Your woman?" Her eyes twinkled with mirth.

"Got a problem with that?"

"Not really."

"Good."

"Look at you two," Ally teased.

"Nice to see you Ally," Matt said. "What would you like, Jordan?"

She gave him a look that reminded him of her temper since she clearly didn't like being teased. Damn, it was good to be back. "I'd like a Diet Coke and some of that pot roast I smell. It made my stomach rumble as soon as we walked in."

Ally nodded. "I swear I could gain ten pounds just smelling it. What about you, Matt?"

"Same thing for me but make mine a Coke."

"Be back with your drinks." Ally hurried off and went to another table. That woman worked too hard, and Matt wished there was something he could do about it. Short of handing her money— which she would never accept—he came up with nothing.

"She's doing okay, isn't she?" Jordan asked in a hushed voice.

Matt shook his head. "I don't quite know."

"Damn, I was afraid of that."

"My brothers and I are watching out for her.

She and her kids will never go hungry or homeless, but I wish there was a way we could ease her burden."

"You're a good man, Matt Cooper."

He kissed her nose and wrapped his arm around her shoulders. "You're not too bad yourself, Jordan Cross."

"Ah, good to find the two of you here. Together," Prescott sneered as he walked toward them.

Fuck, this whole routine was getting old.

"Prescott." Matt gave the man a head-tilt. He didn't want to cause a scene and beat the man to a bloody pulp while the asshat cried for his momma. "To what do I owe this pleasure?" Okay, that sounded a bit sarcastic. Sue him.

"I just wanted to give you an update on my project."

Matt squeezed Jordan's shoulder as she stiffened. "Yes?"

Prescott fiddled with his too-shiny tie. "I've put the vote on the agenda for the next council meeting. The fate of *both* houses will be decided then. But don't get your hopes up. I'm not the only one who wants those monstrosities gone. It's time we cleaned up our trash." The bastard turned to Jordan, and Matt wanted to kill him. Slowly.

"Sadly, you aren't able to vote, Jordan, since you aren't a town member."

Matt held both of them back from slapping the smug look from the prick's face.

"Actually, Prescott," Jordan said, "I *can* vote. I'm the sole owner of my grandmother's house, which is a historic town property. That gives me the *right* to vote for my home."

As much as Matt was proud of her for standing up for herself, he had to try hard not to put too much emphasis in the fact that she'd called it her home.

Prescott waved his hand around. "Fine, whatever you want, witch."

Matt stood and went nose to nose with the fucker, but Jordan held him back a bit so he wouldn't actually kill the man.

"Don't push me, Matt. You may have some pull because of your name and the fact that my sister has put her delusional hopes on you, but remember, I'm the mayor."

"You need to walk away from our table. Now," Matt growled.

"Whatever. Just remember your place." With that, he flounced out of the diner.

Matt seethed, his blood boiling. "What do

you say we take our meals to go?" He looked around the quiet diner as the customers did their best to look like they hadn't just witnessed the very public scene.

"Sounds good."

"I'll go pack it up now," Ally said, anger across her face as well. "Thanks for not hitting him here. But I'll help hold your coat later if you want."

Matt laughed, the tension easing out of him a bit. "Thanks for that."

Ally smiled and gave them their bags. "No problem."

He paid, leaving a huge tip, and walked to his Chevy, Jordan by his side.

"Want to eat in my apartment?" he asked after they'd sat in silence for a few minutes.

"I'd like that. I've never seen your place."

He shrugged as he pulled out onto the road in the direction of the hardware store. "It's not much, just a small one-bedroom apartment above my store."

"But it's yours." Her voice held such awe and pride that he fell just that much more in love with her. Dangerous.

"I'd like more one day."

"I know what you mean." Such a wistful tone. That little part of him that made bad decisions wanted to hope she'd give up this notion of leaving and make her home here...with him.

But he couldn't force her. She was as independent as any badass chick. Which was why he loved her because she was so different from him, but so his.

When they arrived and walked upstairs, he led her through the front door, set their food on the counter, and watched her reaction. She surveyed the room, her hands on her hips and a frown on her face.

"What?" he asked, utterly confused at her reaction.

"It isn't what I was expecting." She sat down on his couch, undid her boots—*sexy*—and crossed her legs.

He put their food on the coffee table and sat next to her, loving the way her body settled close to his. "What were you expecting? A bachelor pad?"

"I don't know. It was a cross between something art deco and flashy and a locker room." She smiled wryly and took a bite of her mashed potatoes. He watched her tongue dart out to lick the plastic fork, and he bit back a groan.

He looked around his home with its browns

and soft creams, comfy couches, and pictures of his family on the walls. Not at all what she had imagined. He shrugged. "I like my home. I don't like clutter, and I'm not a sleaze." With that, he took a bite of his pot roast. "Oh God, I think I've died. They out did themselves this time."

Jordan laughed then took another big bite. "Okay, eat first and savor. We can talk later."

"Deal."

When they were finished, he threw away the containers, grabbed a couple of beers, and sat back on the couch. He took a long pull from his, utterly content to sit in silence with Jordan in his arms. He thought, though, if she didn't quit rubbing against him like that, he might have to change their positions and see if her skin still tasted like ripe berries.

Damn erection.

"You're warm," she whispered, her words trailing tingles down his skin.

"Better to warm you with, my dear," he teased.

She leaned up and pressed her lips to his. He put down his beer, did the same to hers, then framed her face in his hands. He pulled back, his breath quickening.

"I like kissing you," she moaned, her lips

wet, begging for him to nibble—so he did.

"I like kissing you too." He sucked in her bottom lip then bit it. She gasped, and he laved the sting. She shifted, and he pulled her onto his lap so her core was right above his dick. When she rolled her hips, he let out a groan.

"Happy to see me, are you?"

His cock saluted, and he smiled. "God, yes." He let his hands trail up her back underneath her shirt, her skin scalding hot against his palms.

They kissed, licked, and nibbled, their moans loud in his quiet apartment. He held her tighter, and she pulled back.

"I can't sleep with you tonight, Matt," she whispered, a frown on her face.

Though he wanted to groan, he held back his tongue. "I know, baby. This is only our first date."

She smiled. "This time."

"This time. But we don't want to rush. I understand. My cock may explode, but it'll be okay."

She rested her head against his. "I'm sorry I'm such a tease."

He pulled her back so he could kiss her

softly. "You're not a tease. You're a woman who knows what she wants. Don't worry. There will be plenty of time for this." He held back a wince at the reminder that they *didn't* have much time, but he ignored it. "What do you say we watch an old Hitchcock movie and hide under a blanket?"

"As long as you keep your hands to yourself." She winked. "Mostly."

"Sounds good to me, baby." He kissed her nose and got the movie ready. They sat in the dark, wrapped in each other as the first scream pierced the room from the TV. He wouldn't rush her, but he didn't want to let go of this. And, frankly, he shouldn't have to. Maybe it was time to figure out just how to keep his Jordan here to stay. Because if she left, he didn't know what he was going to do.

Chapter 6

"Why is it the smell of crayons always reminds me of school?" Jordan asked as she sorted another section of half-used crayons into its colored bin for Abby. "I mean, I get the fact that we used them in school, but I used them outside of it as well."

They were in Abby's classroom going through boxes of school supplies to give to the after school art program that Jordan had volunteered to help with. She loved working with the kids, and some of the parents had even started to warm up to her. Jordan would have rather been reading her spell book or working on her house, but Abby had needed her.

Well, maybe not for the mundane activity of sorting, but the moments where they could just sit and talk to each other were few and far between. Sometimes they just needed some girl time to talk about the men in their lives or, rather, trip over that thin line where they didn't *actually* talk about them but merely alluded to them—because Jordan didn't know what was going on with her and Matt. One minute they were trying to be friends without talking about their past. The next minute they were humping each other on her couch. Not that it wasn't great humping—because it was. She held back a sigh. Fabulous humping. But she didn't know if they'd go further than that. She was leaving... wasn't she?

"Okay, stop thinking in your head and think aloud," Abby said as she closed a full plastic container for crayons that were beyond salvaging for her classroom but could be used in the art room and be melted down for different types of art..

Jordan raised a brow. "I thought the whole point of thinking was to do it in your head. Plus, even if I am thinking aloud, I have to think of it in my head first. Your logic is flawed." She bit her lip to hold back a smile. God, she loved teasing Abby because the other woman did it right back. Their words weren't malicious with hidden meanings. Jordan would never harp on Abby's lack of boyfriend, and Abby would never harp on the fact that Jordan was a witch...unlike the rest of the girls in town.

Freaking Stacey...

"Just shut up. You think you can get around telling me what's making you look like you lost your best friend by pretending to be on *Dawson's Creek* and talking your way out of it."

"Oh my God, did you just use a *Dawson's Creek* reference? It's been off the air for like a decade."

Abby blushed and straightened another box of crayons. "I've been watching it on Netflix at night."

"Okay, we need to get you out more."

"I can't help it." Abby batted her eyelashes and stared off into space dreamily.

"If you're picturing Dawson right now, I'm going to smack you."

Abby looked appalled, and Jordan laughed. "Heck, no. Joshua Jackson's Pacey all the way. Besides, Dawson always looked like his head was blown up wrong or something, like Frankenstein's monster." Abby tilted her head and gave her a serious expression as if their conversation had any merit in the real world.

Jordan burst out laughing until tears fell

down her cheeks and her side ached.

"Oh, God, I needed that. True, Pacey was dreamy. I'll give you that. I used to make Matt watch it with me." That familiar ache settled around her heart, but it wasn't as painful as it usually was. Maybe because she was thinking about actually getting horizontal with the man?

And then her stomach turned. Oh yeah, then she was leaving, probably not the best avenue for her thoughts to take.

"Okay, for the love of God, tell me what you're thinking. I'm using my best stuff over here and you're only laughing for like a minute." Abby shifted on the little kindergarten seat, her body too big for the seat, but she still looked cuter than Jordan did with her long legs wrapped around two of them.

Jordan let out a breath, not wanting to talk about her love life. Or the fact that she even had a love life, considering the whole point of coming to Holiday was to find *herself*...not a man.

Stupid, stupid Cooper men and their sweaty bodies when they took off their shirts while they worked on her house.

"I think I love Matt," she blurted out, trying to get the image of her tongue running down the hard ridges on his abs out of her mind. She could practically taste the salty goodness. *Bad Jordan.*

Abby blinked. "And?"

Jordan stood quickly, the little chairs sliding in every direction. "What do you mean *and*? I just told you I was in love with my old boyfriend, and all you can say is *and*? What the hell?"

Abby straightened and moved the chairs back in place. "Jordan, it's not a secret. Anyone could have told you that you loved him. I'm pretty sure Matt could have too, though he wouldn't because he's an honorable man. You two were childhood sweethearts who didn't get a chance to see where things would go. Your story is a legend in this town. Even I heard about it, and I was a few years behind you in school. It's only natural that you'd come back and find yourself in love with him."

Jordan crossed her arms over her chest, annoyed. She wasn't that transparent, was she? Damn.

"The question is," Abby continued, "what are you going to do about it?"

Jordan waved her hands in the air, holding back the tears that wanted to come with her frustration. "I don't know. That's the problem. Don't you see? I can't stay here, Abby. I can't."

Jordan sat down on Abby's desk chair and wrapped her arms around her knees, her memories trying to take hold, but she couldn't let them.

"Talk to me, Jor." Abby knelt before her, her eyes pleading. "Tell me what happened. Why did you leave?"

"I can't." Jordan's voice broke, and she shook her head. "Not yet."

Abby nodded and brushed a lock of hair from Jordan's face. "Okay, then tell me something else. Anything. Ease your burdens. It's what I'm here for."

Jordan took a deep breath and wiped her eyes. She hated crying, hated looking weak. It was a real indicator of how much she liked and trusted Abby that she'd broken down in front of her. Or maybe she just needed to cry a bit. Most likely, it was a mixture of both.

"What do you want to know?"

"Well, since you won't tell me what is really bothering you, why don't you talk to me about being a witch?"

Jordan froze, a metallic taste on her tongue. She didn't talk about her craft with *anyone*. She used to be able to talk about it somewhat with Matt, but now she was afraid to. She'd seen the look in his eye when they'd talked about it before. It hurt, but she could work with it. Being a witch was who she was. Or who she was supposed to be.

Abby bit her lip and shook her head. "I'm

sorry. That was crass, wasn't it? Damn. I didn't mean to make you feel worse. I'm just interested, you know?"

"Because I'm a freak?" Jordan bit out, angry at herself more than Abby. Why did she let herself get into situations like this? She should have known better. Any time she got close to someone in this God-forsaken town, they turned on her. They all wanted to know more about the witch and her powers and what she could do for them. If one of the townsfolk wasn't scared she'd put a hex on them, they wanted to be her buddy so they could get a charm or a spell for themselves.

"What? No! That's not what I meant at all." Abby stood, her eyes watering. "I just know you're a witch. I want to know things first-hand, rather than just what I've heard. It's a part of you, and you never talk about it. I thought you'd want to since we're friends. I mean I'm here for you."

Jordan knew better. People didn't want to know about her. No, they wanted to know what she could do for them. She'd seen it all before. She'd thought she'd known better this time about who she could befriend. Apparently not.

The best defense was a good offense. "Let me guess. What could you want from me? Maybe a love spell? Can't get a man on your own, huh? So you had to come to the witch to get help?"

Abby paled, tears streaming down her

cheeks. "Jordan..." Her voice cracked, and she backed up.

God, she knew she was overacting; she fucking knew it. Abby had done nothing wrong, but Jordan couldn't stop. Years of frustration poured out of her. "Well, I'm sorry. There's nothing I can do for you. You're destined to be a virgin forever, aren't you?" Energy pooled around her, her fingers sparking as magic swirled. She tamped it down, or at least tried to.

The unused magic in her system—the kind she'd been hiding since that fateful night eleven years ago—seeped out, ignited by her anger. Her magic had always been controlled by her emotions. It seemed, this time, her magic was the one fueling her emotions.

"Jordan, stop it, please," Abby pleaded.

"I can't get you Tyler, Abby. I can't. I don't know why you even tried being my friend, but I can't create love with magic and supply you a lover. Get a man on your own."

"That's enough, Jordan."

Tyler's deep voice startled her, and her magic kicked up a notch at the sound, emitting a flame that licked the room, leaving a scorch mark on the wall.

She deflated, her body going back to

normal. It was if the magic within her had built up with its lack of use and turned into something nasty and cruel. That wasn't her. That couldn't be her. "Oh, God, Abby. I'm so sorry." She reached out to the other woman, tears running down her cheeks. What had she done?

Abby shook her head, her gaze on Tyler. Oh, fuck. How much had he heard? Damn, she hadn't meant to say anything. She liked Abby. Fuck.

Abby wiped her eyes and straightened her shoulders before walking to the door.

"Abigail..." Tyler whispered as she walked past him, his hand out as if to touch her. Abby walked faster, not listening. When she left, Jordan sank to the floor, her mind rolling and her body shaking.

Oh, God. She hadn't meant to do that.

"You have a lot of fucking nerve, Jor. Fucking nerve." Tyler walked in the room, his gun on his hip and his sheriff's badge gleaming in the light. She gulped. She knew he wouldn't use his gun, but it burned a hole in her. She had a weapon of her own, and she'd used it in anger. What was wrong with her? "I should arrest you right now for what you did to Abby. You didn't control your magic and you could have killed her."

"Tyler...what you heard..." How was she going to fix this?

"No, shut it. I don't want to hear it. Abigail has been nothing but nice to you. She already faces a lot of flak in this town because she doesn't talk to everyone. She's quiet, Jordan. Nice. Don't you realize that? She's your friend. Or was your friend. Because, after that little show, I wouldn't be surprised if she didn't join Stacey's version of a welcoming committee and kick your ass out of town. I just might join her." Tyler's eyes turned cold as his anger radiated off him in waves.

"I don't know what came over me, Ty." She looked at the sheriff, who was also the easy- to-laugh ladies' man. But she didn't see that side of him now. No, the man who smiled and laughed was gone. In his place, stood a man blazing with pure white-hot anger.

"You could have fucking killed her. Do you realize that? You don't have your magic in check, and you fucked it up. You might have killed the only woman who can stand to talk to you."

Talk about twisting the knife, but she deserved it. Her insecurities about her identity were apparently greater than she'd thought. She was the worst of the worst and felt like something on the bottom of someone's shoe. She didn't deserve anything. Not Matt, not friends...not anything.

"Get your mind out of your own fucking pity party. I'm so tired of this, Jordan." Tyler strode to the sink in the back and ripped open the cabinet.

He got out some rags and a bucket then filled it with hot water and soap. He stormed back, the water sloshing over the sides.

"Help me clean up this fucking mark since you caused it. I don't want Abigail to have to look at it when she comes back." He started scrubbing the wall with a force that scared Jordan.

Who was this man? Not the laid-back guy who'd always had a smile for her.

"I'm so sorry, Tyler."

He shook his head. "It's not me who you should be apologizing to. I can't believe you said that to her. She'd been nothing but kind to you. So what if she doesn't date? It's not your place to judge. I thought your place was to stand by her against the people who use tactics like the ones you just used, but apparently, I was wrong."

"I don't know why I did it."

"Shut up. You do know why." He scrubbed harder, and she joined him, her tears falling as she cleaned up the soot from her magic.

She'd never lost control like that before, and it scared her more than she'd like to admit.

"You need to get your head on straight, Jor. You walk around like you don't care about what people say about you. But you do. If you didn't, this wouldn't have happened. You're wound so tight your magic can't come out and breathe. You don't know how to control it because you don't practice."

She gulped, shame washing over her. "How would you know? How do you know so much about this?" Tyler wasn't a witch, of that much she was certain.

"I don't know about being a witch, but I do know about being responsible, and you're not owning up to it. I know you don't plan on staying here, and as much as that will kill Matt, I don't want you here if you're going to be a danger to my people."

Jordan staggered back, hurt sliding through her. "What?"

"You heard me. Get your act together, Jor. One day you'll have even less control than you had today and you'll hurt someone, maybe even kill them. I don't want it to be Matt or someone else I care about it. I love you like a sister, Jor, and I don't want to see you hurt."

Jordan ran her hand through her hair, her body tired from exertion and her emotions. "I don't know why I reacted like that," she whispered.

"You do know. You just need to figure out what you're going to do about it."

They cleaned the last of the soot off in silence, guilt over her actions eating at her.

"What am I going to tell her, Ty?"

He shook his head, his jaw set. "I don't know, but you better make it good. She deserves more than what she's getting from this town."

Jordan nodded, her teeth biting into her lip.

"You do too, Jor. But right now? You're not going to get it. Own up to yourself and maybe others will see what Matt does."

He left without another word, and Jordan sank down into one of the little chairs. She'd almost killed someone she cared about because she couldn't control her magic. She'd been afraid, afraid that she'd be asked to do something she didn't want to do with a power she didn't understand. The only people who'd never asked anything of her had been the Coopers...and Abby. Yet she'd over-reacted because she was a screw-up.

She closed her eyes, her body too tired to think. She needed to fix this with Abby. Then maybe fix herself, because when she moved away, she didn't want to kill a stranger. And if by some stroke of luck she stayed, she didn't want to kill someone she loved.

Chapter 7

"Damn it. Why isn't there a book called *What to Do if You're Turned into a Ghost*?" Matt slammed the thick volume shut as dust rose up from the old book. He rubbed his eyes with the heels of his hands and cursed again.

Reading old texts he'd borrowed from the library wasn't getting him anywhere. For the past eleven years, he'd been researching what he could do to fix his problem. He snorted. Yeah, problem. What a small word to explain he was a freaking ghost five days a month. No matter what he read, though, nothing seemed to be close to what he dealt with.

There were legit texts that said the souls of the deceased had unfinished business left on this plane and therefore couldn't move on. That sounded a bit like every movie he'd ever seen...but it had been worth a try so he'd tried to finish every unfinished piece of business he might have. Even though he wouldn't have been quite ready to move on at his age regardless, he'd still finished his degree, bought his business, and tried his best to accomplish most of his goals. He'd even made sure he kept on his brothers' good sides.

The fact that he hadn't married, had kids, or resolved things with Jordan seemed to be the only major goals left untouched. But even then... would he move on? He wasn't even sure he could have kids, and he wasn't sure he should bring some poor, unsuspecting woman into his nightmare. So, he was pretty sure that, even though the texts had offered him a possible solution, it wasn't the right path for him.

Other books said that he'd chosen this. He snorted. Right, like he'd have chosen to be connected to a building that no one wanted and which the entire town desired to tear down. He certainly wouldn't have chosen to go through agonizing pain every month when he shifted or faded or whatever the hell he wanted to call it. No, he hadn't chosen this. The texts that said he'd chosen this so he could watch over this plane or because he was too scared to move on weren't right about his case.

He wouldn't have chosen this for anything.

As he flipped through the pages, he started to doubt his sanity. Were there others in the world that he hadn't known about? Other ghosts? What about other...things? He'd always known Jordan was a witch and had never questioned it. It was a part of her, and therefore, something he'd understood at the time, but he'd never really thought past that. Stupid really. In retrospect, he should have thought about past magic and what else went bump in the night.

But, nightmares weren't real. At least that was what he'd always thought. Now that he was a ghost though...what if he'd been wrong? What else might be out there?

Everything he'd read pointed to their existence. But what did a ghost like him do?

No matter what he read, these books wanted him to move on. To realize he wasn't alive anymore. That he was dead.

Funny, he didn't actually *remember* dying.

But was he dead? He was alive for twenty-five days out of the month, so he couldn't actually be dead. When he was in the real world, he felt just as alive as he had before the incident. He could touch; people could touch him. He had feelings, so his body worked. What could cause him to be part alive and part dead? Why was he able to live in the real world most of the time, but was forced to live in the ghost world part of the time?

He clenched his fists and took a deep breath, trying to convince himself he was truly alive. He could breathe. His lungs burned, and he fought off the wave of nausea that always came whenever he thought about the fact that he was probably dead.

He didn't want to be dead. He'd barely had a chance to live. He'd been dealing with this crap since he was eighteen and just now had the desire to actually make it past *living* from day-to-day. He wanted Jordan.

For now. Forever.

Or at least, he *wanted* to want Jordan. He couldn't get past the betrayal of her leaving and her part in his predicament because, for all his research, he still had a pretty good idea that only magic could have done this to him.

And he only knew one witch that could have done it.

Jordan.

Was it mere coincidence that he'd turned into a ghost for the first time on the night she'd left town—and him?

He closed his eyes and tried not to think about that first night. He hadn't even known she had left until the next morning. No, that night he'd been at the Marlow place, waiting for her. When he'd found out she'd left, he'd felt as if someone had punched him in the stomach then thrown him against the wall. He'd broken out in a sweat, his vision going hazy. Then he'd looked down at his hands...

He swallowed the bile in his throat then took a deep breath. After some time had passed, he'd finally been able to deal with the sensation and the pain of his body fading into nothingness, but the idea still scared the shit out of him.

What if one day he didn't come back?

What if he faded to his ghost form and just...stayed there?

Okay, he needed to stop thinking about crap like that. It wasn't getting him anywhere. He opened another book, rubbed his eyes, and re-read another chapter. It had occurred to him in the past that, if he'd just asked for help, he wouldn't feel as lost as he did.

But whom could he ask?

As much as he loved Holiday, he didn't trust the town with this secret. He'd seen the way they'd treated Jordan when she'd been outed as a witch. Though he'd done all he could to protect her, it hadn't been enough. After all, she'd left.

He could have told his brothers countless times. In fact, he almost had every time the moon started to grow and he knew his days as a solid were numbered. But he could never gain the courage to come out say and he was a ghost.

They'd already lost so much with their parents' deaths and having to grow up too fast. He hadn't been able to put anything else on their shoulders.

God, he felt like a coward. He leafed through another text, his gaze straying to articles about séances, spells, and resurrection. He looked at the clock and grimaced. Only a couple more hours before he faded again. It was two days before Halloween and the full moon, so tonight was the first night of his curse. He turned another page, willing it to have the answers.

No such luck.

He'd find something. He had to because, if he didn't, he didn't know how much longer he could live not being alive.

****

Jordan stood on Abby's front porch, a box of homemade sugar cookies in one hand, still warm from the oven, and a bouquet of flowers in the other. She looked like she was picking up her date for a Valentine's Day dance, not like a woman ready to grovel to the only woman in the world who cared about her.

She held the flowers a bit tighter and bit her lip. God, she couldn't believe she'd reacted like that to Abby's innocent question. She'd almost killed her friend, and all because she'd been too insecure to talk it out without being a bitch.

The look on Tyler's face...

God. She'd most likely lost Tyler and Abby for good. Frankly, if the two of them gave up on her, she deserved it. She rocked from foot to foot, unease creeping through her.

Why was she here? This wasn't going to work. She closed her eyes, her magic pulsating through her. That was the *one* thing she couldn't let happen. She couldn't let her magic run away with her again. She had to learn to tame it. Control it. Own it.

Tyler was right.

She was scared.

She'd have to learn to control her magic and be okay with it. If she didn't, she might hurt someone she cared about...or kill them.

Right now, she had to do something even more important. Apologize. She didn't deserve forgiveness, and Abby could very well slam the door in her face, but she needed to say she was sorry.

God, sorry was such a small word, often meaningless in most situations, but she still needed to say it. Abby deserved at least that.

The door opened and Abby looked at her with a frown on her face. "Are you going to stand out here in the wind for thirty more minutes before you actually ring the bell? Or do you just like to adorn front porches in your downtime?" Abby asked, her hair in a cute ponytail on the top of her head. She wore tight yoga pants and a tank top and looked like she had just been working out.

"Hi, Abby." And now she needed to say something. Anything. And....nothing.

"Oh God, you brought cookies?"

Jordan nodded, nervous. She held out the box and flowers, her head down. She really sucked at this.

"You might as well get out of the cold and come in."

Jordan looked up, and Abby walked in, leaving her alone on the porch. She looked around and shrugged. Maybe Abby wanted to kill her in private. She walked in, closed the door behind her, and took off her coat.

Abby lived in a small, one-bedroom house that sat on a large amount of acreage so she could add on if she ever wanted to. Inside, the house personified home and warmth, filled with comfy couches and chairs—the kind you wanted to sink into and take a nap. Knick-knacks seemed to be everywhere, but the house wasn't cluttered.

It looked like a home that desperately needed a family.

Jordan held back a sob, remembering what she'd said to Abby about her lack of a love life. She deserved to be drawn and quartered in the center of town.

"Okay, it's official. I'm ruining my diet with one of these cookies," Abby said as she walked back into the room, a nervous smile on her face. "They're still warm and everything." She bit into one and moaned. "You're bad for me, Jordan Cross."

Jordan hiccupped a sob. "I know, Abby. I'm so, so sorry for what I said and did. I didn't mean it."

Abby lowered her head and sank into her couch, cookie forgotten.

"Abby?" Jordan knelt in front of her, her hands shaking.

"I know I'm not pretty. I know that, Jor. I know that I don't have a chance with Tyler, or any man in Holiday for that matter. I just thought you understood that I didn't want to talk about it."

Tears slid down both of their faces, and Jordan took Abby's hands in a firm grip. "You are beautiful, Abby."

The other woman shook her head vehemently. "Stop it. Just stop trying to make me feel better."

"I'm not going to stop. You have curves to die for."

"I'm fat."

"No, you're not. You're just not anorexic or fake."

Abby let out a snort.

"You're beautiful. Men look at you, Abby, once you let them."

"What is that supposed to mean?"

"Most men see you as their friend, Abby."

"If they even see me at all."

Jordan shook her head. "Then that's their problem. You could have any man you wanted if you tried. But I know you're holding out for someone."

Abby looked into her eyes and gave a weak smile. "I know Tyler will never see me. I'm okay with that."

Jordan's heart broke for her. "Don't be. He saw you yesterday."

Abby gave out a hollow laugh. "Yeah, it only took you almost killing me to do it."

Pain lanced through her. "I am so, so sorry, Abby."

"Oddly enough, that part I can forgive, Jordan. You didn't mean to do it. You just need to learn to control it better. And you will, won't you?" Abby looked at her with a pointed look, and Jordan lowered her head.

"I'm going to try," she whispered.

"Don't try, do."

They laughed, and Jordan shook her finger at her. "Okay, Yoda."

Abby blushed. "Oh God, don't let Tyler know I'm a geek too."

"Hey, I knew it was a *Star Wars* reference too."

"Yeah, but you already have Matt. Your

geekiness won't get in the way of getting a man."

Her stomach ached, and Jordan moved to sit next to her friend. Everything seemed to roll into one, what she'd done to Abby, how her relationship with Matt was progressing...her entire life. "I don't know about that."

"Tell me about it." She handed her a cookie and took a bite.

Jordan licked the frosting off—mmm, goodness—and tried to put into words what her body had been telling her for years.

"I almost hurt you because I'm afraid to be a witch."

"I know, hon."

Jordan resisted the urge to roll her eyes. "How is it you and Tyler knew that, and I didn't?"

Abby blanched a bit at Tyler's name, and Jordan immediately regretted saying his name. "Sorry, Abby. I'll quit talking about him."

Abby shook her head. "No, you need to say his name, and I need to get over it."

Jordan gave Abby another cookie and didn't go further on that subject. "Okay, so I need to figure out how to be a witch."

Abby smiled. "You already know, Jordan.

It's in you."

"Then why do I suppress it?"

"Because you're scared."

Jordan looked at her hands and watched as sparks radiated out from the tips. Unlike the manic energy from the day before, these were warm and loving. Like little balls of light that sparkled and knew they were in the right place. She should have been surprised by what she was seeing, but she wasn't. Her magic was tied to her emotions, she'd known that. But she hadn't been taking care of herself, so she couldn't control it. She looked at the little balls of light and sighed, they were right. This was what her magic was supposed to be. Controlled and loved.

Why couldn't all her magic act like that?

Abby held her hands out tentatively, and Jordan watched as the little sparks danced to her friend's hands and circled them.

Abby gasped. "It tickles," she said with a laugh.

"Really? It only feels like I'm meditating or something. Like I'm at peace and happiness is settling through me. It's warm, sort of like a nice spring day after a long frost."

"It's really cool, Jordan. Whenever the little balls touch me, yes, it tickles, but it's like a connection to you, you know? It's like you're sharing yourself. I like it."

"I'm glad you feel safe, Abby."

"I feel safe because I trust you." The magic dissipated, and she smiled. "I know you got scared, and that's why you lashed out. Hence why I forgive you. Though the cookies help."

Jordan smiled and took another cookie.

"But, Jordan, you have to talk about it."

"Talk about what?"

"What's it like being a witch. You need to talk about it to come to terms with how you feel about it. Once you do that, maybe you'll have control. Besides, I want to know how it affects you, how you feel, what you'd like to be able to do with it."

Jordan froze. It was the same question Abby had asked before, only then it had made her blow her top off and lose control. This time she felt calm, and she also knew it was time to share herself.

"Being a witch is hereditary. My mother, grandmother, and so on were all witches, though our powers are all unique in strength and variety. My mother barely had any power, and my grandmother only had a bit more in terms of healing. They had thought the bloodline was being diluted. Then I was born. Apparently, I have the strongest powers in centuries. I could, with practice, do any kind of spell in any kind of discipline, something that is highly unheard of. At least that's what my grandmother had said." And why they'd fought. Her grandmother had wanted her to pursue her magic and be a true witch while Jordan had only wanted to be normal. That had fractured their relationship to the point that even thinking about doing magic made Jordan want cry. It wasn't fair that now she was starting to believe in herself, her grandmother wasn't here to share it. As a child, she'd used her magic more, but then had cut herself off from it when the taunting had started.

"That's amazing, Jordan. But why didn't you use it?" Abby said, breaking into her thoughts.

"Because when I was five, I made a flower bloom, and Stacey saw me. She ran directly to her perfectly normal mom and dad and tattled. They in turn told their friends and everyone who would listen that I was a danger to their children. Kids stopped playing with me and started to pick on me. The Coopers were the only ones who stood by me." She held back the rage that usually came with that memory. The damned nosey bitch had ruined her life. "I quit using magic after that." Damn, why had she let Stacey hold so much power over her? Why was she *still* allowing Stacey to do that?

"And that's how everyone knew you were a witch."

"Pretty much. I mean our family has always been oddballs. People have been spreading rumors for decades. But it wasn't until then that my mistake confirmed it."

"You were five, Jor. Cut yourself a little slack."

"But if I hadn't—"

"No, stop right there. You can't live in the past. You can't change it. But you can move on."

Jordan closed her eyes. "I don't know if I can."

"You can if you ask for help. I mean I'm not a witch, but I'm a quick study. I can help you meditate, look through books, whatever. You need to learn control and with more knowledge that can happen. I'm a teacher, I know these things. I'll do anything, Jor. Just let me know what I can do."

Happiness and relief filled her. God, she'd almost lost this perfect woman as her best friend because she was a freaking idiot.

She pulled Abby into a hug and laughed. "I don't know what I'd do without you."

"Don't think about it. I'm here if you're here."

"You *will* figure out how to be a witch, Jordan. You're strong and willing to gain control. I believe in you."

Jordan smiled and hugged her friend closer.

"Crap! Is that the time?" Abby vaulted from the couch and ran to her room.

"What's going on?" Jordan stood up and cleaned up their mess as Abby stripped down and pulled on a pair of slacks and a nice top.

"Sorry for stripping in front of you, but I have to go. I promised Justin I'd be at the school to help him get the rest of the sets ready for the Halloween play at the school."

"If you're doing that, why are you putting on nice clothes?"

"Because Justin is the principal?"

"Try again."

Abby let out a sigh as she tried to do her hair. "Because Prescott will be there watching us to make sure it's up to *his* standards. I hate that I even care what he thinks, but he controls the purse strings. I hate Holiday sometimes. It's so backwards in the way it does things." She rolled her eyes and put on mascara at the same time—talented.

Jordan's stomach clenched at the reminder of Prescott but ignored it. "I'll let myself out then. Good luck, hon."

Abby gave a forced smile. "Thanks, I'm going to need it."

Jordan got in her Mustang and found herself driving toward the other end of town where the old Marlow place stood. For some reason, she'd always felt drawn to the place, at least since she'd come back to Holiday. As the sun started to set, she parked in front of it. She only wanted to go inside to see if anything remained. She didn't want Prescott to tear it down. This place was a landmark...even if people said it was haunted.

She smiled. Maybe tonight she'd see her ghost.

Jordan walked through the unlocked door and froze, her heart racing.

"Jordan..." Matt whispered.

She blinked as he stood in the foyer as the last rays of the sun went below the horizon. The hairs on the back of her neck stood up as she watched his body fade from vision.

Oh, God. Matt Cooper was the Old Marlow Ghost.

Oh, shit.

Chapter 8

Matt's worst nightmare stood in front of him, her gaze never straying from him. Or rather, her gaze locked *through* him. Fucking shit. He hadn't expected Jordan to be here tonight.

How was he supposed to deal with this? What should he say?

Fuck.

"Matt?" she whispered, her lower lip trembling.

Oh, shit, she couldn't cry. He wouldn't be able to handle it. Yeah, he, like most men, couldn't handle women crying, but he *definitely* couldn't handle the tears that were flooding Jordan's eyes right now.

He took a deep breath—something really fucking odd to do when he was a ghost because everything was about fifty degrees cooler in this form—and nodded.

"Yeah, baby. It's me."

Subtle. Nice.

"You're a...you're..." She blinked again and looked a little unsteady on her feet. Fuck, he couldn't touch her to help her.

"A ghost," he finished for her. "I find it easier to just say it rather than beat around the bush. That doesn't make it any less real."

She lowered herself to the floor, her face a bit awestruck, her eyes wide, and her mouth open. "How...when?"

"I don't know how, baby." He held a hand up to her and traced her jaw about two inches away from her face.

"Cold..."

He swiped his hand back and cursed. "I'm sorry."

She gulped and shook her head, visibly

pulling herself together, though tears still filled her eyes. "You can't touch me, can you?"

He gave a weak smile and shook his head. "No, I can't."

"But you're touching the floor. How is that possible?"

"I can touch everything in this house. I can also walk through everything if I wanted to, but I have to think about it."

"But what about outside the house?"

"I can't go outside, Jor."

"What do you mean?"

"If I go outside when I'm like this, it's hard to come back from wherever the hell I go. So hard in fact, I might not come back. If I'm not here, then I can't get back to my physical form."

If possible, her eyes widened even more, and she took a shuddering breath. "Matt..." She choked back a sob then shook her head and took a deep breath. "Why didn't you tell me?"

He shook his head, the cool drafts of the house flowing through him and sending chills down his translucent body. "I couldn't, Jor. I haven't been able to tell anyone."

"Your brothers?"

He tried to smile. "No, not even them."

"But you tell each other everything. The Coopers are the closest family I know."

"I can't, Jor."

She wiped her cheeks and nodded. "I understand... I think. I just wish you didn't have to bear this alone."

A slight weight lifted off his shoulders at the thought that she knew and wasn't running. Someone else knew his secret and she was handling it, at least as well as could be expected.

Jordan stood up, walked to the living room, and sat on one of the couches covered with a tarp. Dust flew around her, and she coughed.

"Sorry about that. I haven't been too much into cleaning."

"I wouldn't think so." She straightened her shoulders and got that look she always had when she was trying to figure out a problem, namely, him. He walked toward her and sat next to her. Her eyes widened, but he didn't touch her—couldn't touch her. "Okay, so you said you don't know how you ended up this way. Tell me what you remember. We can get to the bottom of this. I mean...you can't be...de—" She choked off the last word, and Matt wanted to hold her with every ounce of his being.

"So, for five days a month, I'm a ghost. Or whatever the hell I am."

"Five days? Every month? God, that's so much."

He nodded. "Tell me about it. It all revolves around the full moon."

"Oddly enough, that makes a weird sort of sense."

"Only a witch would say that."

"Okay, so I guess it's two days before and two days after."

"Right in one. I need to be here by sunset on those days."

"Or you won't come back or get your physical body back," she whispered, her eyes filling again, but not crying.

"I don't know."

"What do you feel when it happens? I mean what does it feel like to be a ghost?"

He shrugged. "There's a bit of...pain. And cold. Yeah, cold." And lonely.

"I'm so sorry, Matt."

He shook his head but didn't respond. Did she know that she was the culprit? That her leaving must have triggered something? Well, maybe, he didn't know for sure, but he had his guesses. No, why would she?

"When did this first happen?"

His head shot up, and he blinked. "Eleven years ago." There, let her think what she wanted.

"You mean..." Her hands shook, and he had the overwhelming urge to hold them and comfort the woman who'd made him this way. Anger and disappointment flooded him that he couldn't do that.

"Yep. That night I was out here waiting for you. Remember?"

She nodded and bit her lip, the tears freely flowing this time.

"Well, Stacey showed up, and we drank some beer. She left, and I waited. I didn't think much of it at the time. In fact, I didn't really want her there. I knew you two hated each other, with good reason on your part. But you were so late that I thought you weren't coming. And we'd had that fight earlier in the day, I thought I'd be alone all night, I guess. So, I let her stay and we drank. She left, and I waited. When the sun set, I changed for the first time."

"I'm so sorry, Matt."

"I'm a ghost, Jordan. There's nothing you

can really do about it."

"But, Matt, I don't think you're a real ghost."

He looked down at his body—through his body—and gave a dry chuckle. "I think the fact that I can see the couch through my legs begs to differ."

"No, I mean, you didn't die. That means you aren't a real ghost."

A small kernel of hope sprouted in him, but he had to ignore it. "How do you know I didn't die?"

"Wouldn't you have mentioned it? You're alive for over three-quarters of a month at a time. You have a real life, a real physical body and the ability to interact with the real world. You're alive, Matt. You didn't die."

"Maybe I don't remember."

She shook her head. "But you remember everything else about that night. And ghosts don't go walking around in corporeal form in the daylight."

"Maybe I'm special."

"Oh, baby, you're special all right. But you're not a true ghost."

"What does that mean?"

"That means, if we figure out the initial

trigger, we might be able to fix it."

His body shook as his emotions went haywire. Could Jordan fix this? Should he tell her that he blamed her, as irrational as it was?

"How do you know so much about ghosts?"

She shrugged. "I've met a couple ghosts and helped them move on."

His eyes widened. "That wasn't what I was expecting. Is it because you're a witch?"

"I think so. I can sense ghosts more than the average person. I don't like seeing people, even ghosts, walk around sad and without a purpose because they don't know what to do and where to go."

"So you think you can help me?"

"I hope I can. I want you to be okay, Matt. I...I care about you." She wrung her hands together, and Matt took a deep, cool breath.

He loved the woman on this couch, and she only cared about him? Maybe she was just too afraid to say anything else. After all, they hadn't been together in eleven years. A lot could have happened, and did happen, in that time...like him becoming a ghost.

"Hey, why did you come here anyway?"

"Oh, I don't know. I just wanted to, I guess. I felt this pull to come here. Maybe it was you?"

He smiled. "That attracted to me, are you?"

She laughed away the last of her tears, and Matt felt a small victory. "That must be it. Ghost and all."

"Ah, so you do only want me for my body."

"You know it."

He shook his head. "What are your plans now? I don't think hanging out with your ghost boyfriend, or whatever the hell I am, really constitutes fun."

"Boyfriend?"

"Really? That's what you took from that conversation?"

Her smile fell, and she reached for his hands before pulling them back at the last minute. "I'm still leaving, Matt."

Even though he blamed her for his condition, he still wanted her, loved her. She couldn't leave. He had to make her stay.

"One day at a time, Jor."

She nodded but didn't smile. "Okay, then I guess that means I'm not leaving yet."

"What?" His heart raced.

"I'll stay the night," she said quickly as Matt's pulse died down.

Odd that he still could feel his pulse even though he could see through himself. Really weird.

"Yeah? You want to do some other worldly hanky-panky?"

She laughed and almost fell off the couch. "Hanky-panky?"

"Don't knock it until you try it."

She shook her head. "Oh, I know I'd love it. But what century are you from? Hanky-panky?"

"It's Holiday, Montana, Jor. We live to be outdated."

"Okay, I believe you. Now, what is it a ghost like you does when they're all alone in the house?"

He shrugged. "I read, play chess with myself, fix up some of the interior. The tools were already here so I can touch them."

"Wanna have a partner for chess? I'm not that good, but it has to be better than you playing against your right hand."

"Hey, it was my left, and be warned, he's very good."

She laughed and followed him to the parlor where he'd laid the chess board and pieces.

"I'm glad you're here, Jor."

She gave a sad smile and traced a hand over his jaw without touching so she wouldn't go through. Her warmth seeped into him, and he shivered. "I'm glad too."

The urge to grab her and never let go shot through him. Thankfully, his non-corporeal form hindered that. He didn't want to scare her, and his being a ghost was the least of his worries when it came to that. Professing his undying love might do the trick. And that was scary as hell.

****

Jordan cracked open her eyes as the sunlight shone through the slits in the boarded-up window. She'd gone to sleep late the night before after losing to Matt for the eighth time. Apparently, being alone in a spooky house—and being the one who haunted it—made him a really good chess player.

She shifted and froze, forgetting she wasn't alone. An arm wrapped around her waist and cupped her breast. She moaned and smiled.

Ah, now she remembered. She'd fallen asleep on the couch with Matt lying behind her, but not touching. Now that the sun was up, he could touch all he wanted.

She smiled and wiggled her butt as he rocked forward, the bulge in his pants pressing against her.

"Good morning, wicked one."

She curved back into him as he slid his hand under her shirt. He spread his fingers across her belly, and she shivered.

"Good morning, spooky."

He groaned and pulled back from where he was nibbling on her ear lobe. "Really? Spooky? That's the best you can come up with?"

"Sorry, I was distracted."

"Hmm, I think I can distract you some more. What do you think?"

Tendrils of pleasure wove around her, and she tried to turn over. He pulled up and shifted so he was kneeling between her spread legs. She wrapped them around his waist.

"I think you can try."

His eyes darkened, and she traced his unshaven jaw with her finger. She'd done the same the night before but hadn't been able to touch him or feel his skin.

Matt was a ghost.

But her ghost, at least for the time being.

He lowered his head and took her lips. She slid her tongue against his and rocked her hips so she cradled his. He deepened the kiss, their tongues warring with each other. The room filled with the sounds of moans, pleas, and promises.

Her magic pooled in her stomach, her limbs growing heavy as she kissed him. Her body felt like honey was sliding through her; rich, warm honey. Desire and need flooded her. God, she wanted this, wanted him.

He pulled back, both of them breathing heavily. "I want you, Jordan Cross. I want you naked, writhing beneath me. I want to slide into you and feel you clench around me. I want to lick you all over and see what you taste like when you come on my tongue."

She almost came at his words. She moaned and lifted her hips so his erection rubbed against her clit. He smiled and held her hips down. She let out a whimper.

"No you don't, baby. Not until we're clear on one thing."

God, this man drove her crazy, but the good kind of crazy that made her want to strip them down and ride him like a pony.

"What one thing?"

"We're in this together, Jordan. I want you. No stopping. No holding back."

Her body cooled slightly, but she nodded. She could do this. She could. Maybe.

He kissed her softly then stood up.

"Where are you going?" He couldn't leave her now, not like this. Damn man.

Matt smiled and lifted her into his arms and started walking toward another room in the house. "The better question is where are *we* going. Because that couch isn't comfortable. No, I need a better place so I can take you properly."

"Oh, I like it when you think ahead."

He stopped and cursed. "Fuck, I don't have a condom. Damn. Damn. Damn."

He stared to put her down, and she tightened her grip. "It's okay, I'm on the pill."

"Is that enough?" He looked into her eyes,

and she tried to kiss the worries away.

"I'm clean."

"Me too." He let out a breath. "Oh, thank God. I don't think I'd have been able to wait to go to the drug store and get a box. And then there is the whole thing with the gossip of this town. They'd know we were having sex before we actually got to enjoy ourselves."

"Matt?"

"Yes?" he said as he sat her on the dining room table, big and sturdy enough to feed ten people.

"Don't talk about the town when we're about to have sex. It kind of ruins the moment."

He cracked a smile then threw his head back and laughed. "Noted." He stood between her legs, put his palms on the table, and tried to rock it. The table didn't move an inch, and he smiled again. "Good, the table should hold."

Pleasure shot through her. "You want to do it on a table?"

"Yeah, why not?" He kissed her nose. "Come on, you know you've always wanted to."

"What makes you think I haven't?" she teased.

He growled and bit her lip. "Hey, no talking about past lovers when I'm about to strip you naked and make you my breakfast on the table."

Her panties grew damp, and she nodded. "Deal."

He kissed her again, his heady taste dancing on her tongue. She loved this man. Always had, but she couldn't tell him. Not yet.

"Stop thinking so hard," Matt said as he pulled off her top, the cool morning air sending goose bumps up her arms.

He lowered his head and kissed her collarbone. She trailed her hands down his back to the hem of his shirt and tugged. He pulled back and smiled, letting her pull it over his head. She swallowed hard as she took his body in, staring at the lean muscle and those ridges on his abs that begged for her tongue. She leaned forward and kissed the place right above his heart. It beat strong, alive, reminding her that he was here and not a true ghost.

He brushed a lock of hair behind her ear and tilted her head up. She looked into his blue eyes and sighed. He kissed her again, this time unclasping her bra when he did so. Her breasts fell, heavy, needy. He groaned and rolled both nipples with his fingers. Her pussy clenched at his attention, and she scooted to the edge of the table so she could get closer.

"Greedy."

"Shut up and fuck me."

He chuckled deeply. "Anything you want, baby."

He sucked a nipple into his mouth and bit down. She closed her eyes and held back a scream. God, she'd almost come on the spot, and he hadn't even touched her more than a few kisses here and there.

He traced a hand down her stomach and cupped her core. "You're wet, aren't you?" he said once he pulled back, his thumb riding the ridge of her jeans, rasping against her clit.

"Yes, damn it, yes. Please, Matt."

"Oh, I like it when you beg."

"I hate you."

"I know; that's why this is fun."

"Please, Matt."

"There you go with the begging again." He unsnapped her jeans and lowered the zipper but didn't touch her. "I think I should go slower."

"I think if you do, I'll have to take care of things myself."

He groaned. "You know, you'll have to make

yourself come for me one day. But right now, I want a taste."

She smiled and lifted her hips as he took off her jeans and panties in one fluid motion. "Have at it."

He didn't say anything, his gaze on her shaved pussy.

"Matt?" She tried to close her legs, feeling self-conscious.

He gripped her knees and spread her. "Don't move. I'm memorizing to make sure I won't forget."

"Matt..." They were going too slow for her; she needed him. Now. She slid a hand down her stomach and flicked her clit.

"Fuck, Jordan."

He knelt between her legs and licked where she touched, her hips bucking toward his face. He moved her hand so he could get better access, and she shook. He traced her folds with his tongue, his fingers following the path, dipping into her core, and then teasing her clit. Her body felt heavy, needy, and she leaned back on one elbow and used her other hand to play with her nipple.

"Yeah, play with yourself, baby; that's fucking hot."

She smiled and closed her eyes, the sensations too much for her.

"No, keep your eyes open. Watch while I eat you."

She opened them and stared at his dark hair between her pale legs. He sucked, licked, probed, and she rocked. His fingernail scraped against her clit, and she stiffened then came against his face, his name on her lips as she fell onto the table.

She tried to catch her breath, her body warm and tingly, and her magic radiating from her with pleasure. The little balls of light flickered in tiny fireworks and warmth spread through her. Matt gripped her hips again, and she stared at him. He'd stripped down, his cock hard, thick, and pressed against her pussy.

"Ready, baby?"

She nodded, unable to speak. He shifted forward, the tip of his cock sliding between her folds. Fuck, he was big. Bigger than any of the other men she'd dated, yet perfect for her. She watched as he slowly slid into her one inch at a time, her pussy clenching around him as he did so.

When he'd buried himself to the hilt, she moaned. She felt too full, too...everything. She felt like she was on fire, yet shivered. His fingers dug into her hips as he seemed to fight for control.

"Are you okay, baby? Am I hurting you?"

She shook her head, unable to speak.

"We'll go slow, okay? I don't want to hurt you."

She shook her head again. "No, make it fast. You won't hurt me. I trust you."

He groaned and pulled back, her core contracting as he moved. He smiled then rammed into her, his balls slapping against her. She moaned and gripped the edge of the table so she wouldn't move. He pulled out then slammed back in. Her breasts bounced as he did it over and over again, her body rising as she rolled with him, meeting his thrusts. He slid deeper, hitting that spot that made her nerves stand on end. She met his gaze, and she came, her body shaking, cresting, and falling. The magic burst from her with more intensity this time, her body shaking with the delightful pinpricks. He stiffened then shouted her name, her core warming as he came deep inside her.

He fell on top of her yet didn't crush her, their bodies still intimately connected. She held him close, her sweaty limbs too limp to do much more.

"That was..." she whispered.

"Yeah."

"We need to do that again."

He groaned and kissed her. "You're going to kill me, woman."

"But what a way to go."

Chapter 9

Sitting in the armchair, Matt slid his hand up Jordan's thigh and smiled, pleased. They'd made love two more times that morning, and even though he wanted to feel her around him again, he didn't think he was up for it. Literally. After all, he wasn't a kid anymore.

She pushed his hand away and sat up on his lap. "I don't think I can do it again, Matt."

He cupped her breasts and kissed her neck. "I know; I don't think I can either. You've drained me. But I still like touching you."

She wiggled off his lap and smiled at him.

"Oh, I like you touching me too, but if you don't stop, I might just pass out."

"But you'd enjoy it."

She raised a brow and put her hand on her hip. The fierce look was dampened because she was buck naked and sexy as hell. But damn, he could get used to this.

"Hey, buddy. My eyes are up here."

"Yeah, but your breasts are calling to me." He cupped his ear. "You hear that? They're saying 'Matt, we want your lips.' See? I have to answer them."

Jordan groaned and walked toward their pile of clothes. He watched her very bitable ass as she bent to pick up her jeans. He could just make out her pussy when she leaned down far enough. Fuck, apparently he had one more go in him. Who knew?

"Stop staring at my ass, Matt Cooper." She threw his clothes at him and growled playfully.

"But it's a fine ass."

"I work hard to keep it that way, but I can't take another orgasm."

"I could change your mind." Even as he said it, he stood and slid on his jeans and boxers.

"I know you can; hence the reason I'm getting dressed."

"You look like you had a good night."

She groaned again and put her hair up in a ponytail. "Great. Now the whole town will know what I was doing last night. I parked my car in the front so you *know* someone saw it this morning. And even though your car isn't here, I still look all mussed up."

Matt shrugged. "So?"

"You don't care that people will wonder why we got freaky in the haunted house? Wait, no, don't answer that. You'd love for everyone to know we got freaky. It's like some macho guy bull crap. As for the haunted house part, they already think I'm a freak, so they'll just think it's part of my mojo."

He frowned and pulled her into his arms. She sighed but wrapped her arms around his waist. "You're not a freak. And I'm sorry the town sucks ass, but you can't let them get to you."

"Easy for you to say. You keep your special talents a secret. But I understand why you do it."

He kissed the top of her head. "I'm sorry, baby."

"It's okay. I'll get over it. Get your shoes on. I'll take you to breakfast and show the town I don't give a crap. Then we can do some research."

"Research?"

"I want to figure out what happened to make you a ghost. If I do, I can try and fix it."

He nodded while he put on his shoes but didn't say anything. Would she be able to fix something she'd done? He winced inwardly. Okay, so he didn't know she'd actually done it, and the more time he spent with her, the more he thought she couldn't have done it. Maybe it was just a coincidence. But, if that were the case, what would he do? He'd spent eleven years blaming her while still loving her. He didn't know if he could change that.

Glass shattered in the living room, and Jordan screamed. He ran to her as another window broke, the sound of glass skittering against the floor making his skin crawl.

"Jordan? Are you hurt?"

He looked her over and almost tripped. She had cuts down her arms and a large cut on her forehead. Blood seeped from the wounds, and she shook, her magic sparking around her but contained. The little balls of light circled him then settled onto his skin as if they accepted him. Warmth seeped through him in acceptance, as if her magic was a part of him as well.

"What happened? Did your magic do that?"

She looked like she'd been struck and pulled back from him. "What? How could you say that? Someone threw a fucking rock and now I'm bleeding."

Guilt washed over him, and he winced. "I know you wouldn't have done that, Jor. I spoke before I thought. I wasn't thinking."

"I'll say you weren't." She turned away but not before he saw the tears in her eyes.

Fuck. Couldn't he do anything right?

He tried to go to her to wipe off some of the blood and see how bad it was, but she shrugged away. He felt like a total heel.

"I'm okay; it's just a couple of scratches."

"The one on your forehead looks pretty bad. Let me take a look."

"I said I'm fine," she snapped, then closed her eyes. "I'm sorry. I didn't mean to sound like a bitch."

He shook his head. "You're cut and bleeding. It's your prerogative."

She bent down and picked up a jagged rock. "Who do you think threw this?" She clenched the rock in her hand and walked toward the front door.

He grabbed her arm and stopped her. "Hey,

we'll go out together. What if they're still out there? I don't want you to get hurt."

She kissed his jaw, and he took a deep breath. Everything would be okay. It had to.

"It's probably just kids picking on the haunted house as a dare or because they're bored."

"Still doesn't give them the right."

"Oh, I know. Remember what they did to my house?" Her eyes narrowed, and he kissed her nose while looking at the cut on her forehead. It didn't look deep so it probably didn't need stiches, but once they were done looking for whoever did this, he wanted to clean it. The last thing they needed was for it to be infected.

"I remember, baby. Come on, let's go find those punks."

"Punks?" Jordan shook her head and winced. "You've been watching too many cop shows."

Matt shrugged, unrepentant. "I happen to like them."

"Only you."

"You think it's sexy."

"So not the time, Mr. Cooper."

"It's always the time."

She smiled, and he relaxed a bit. He'd only joked around to release the tension in her shoulders, but he was on edge, thinking about whoever was out there. For all he knew, it wasn't some punk kids but something much more dangerous. What, he didn't know, but he didn't want to take chances. He went to the window beside the door and looked through. He saw a kid around fifteen in a red ball cap run around a bush, and Matt groaned.

"Fucking kids."

"See? It's just kids. We can go out, yell, and they'll leave." Jordan gave a wry smile, and Matt shook his head.

"I hope it's that easy."

"They're just kids, Matt. Stupid kids, but they didn't know anyone would be in here."

"Yeah, but we were and your car was parked outside, Jor. It was obvious someone was inside. And you got hurt in the process." Rage built up in him, and he cursed. They'd hurt her, damn it, and he was supposed to go out there and act like a nice guy to get them to leave? Well, too damn bad. If only he were still in his ghost form. He'd scare the shit out of those kids. He smiled. Yeah, that would be nice.

"Uh, Matt, why are you smiling like the Joker from *Batman* right now?"

"Just thinking about how it would be nice to haunt them."

She punched him in the shoulder and scowled. "You're bad."

"True. Okay, come on, let's get this over with."

Matt opened the door and walked out, Jordan hot on his heels. He looked around the barren yard, full of weeds and dead grass, for the culprits but didn't see them. Maybe they'd moved on. Maybe it had been just that one kid.

"You see anyone?" Jordan asked as she looked around his body since he blocked the door.

"Not so far. Maybe they're gone."

"Hopefully. I'm getting hungry."

"I'll feed you, baby. Don't worry."

"Aww, I like it when you go all caveman sometimes. Just don't make it a habit. I'm an independent woman."

He turned around and kissed her. "Wouldn't dream of it because I know you are."

He felt Jordan stiffen, and magic swarmed

around them, this time, not as warm as before, almost protecting, before he heard glass break again. A rock slid past them and he waited for the glass to come inside...but it didn't. He opened his eyes, and she stood in his arms, her eyes focused on something else, something eerie.

He looked behind her, and his jaw dropped. The glass windows on either side of the door had shattered into thousands of little pieces of sparking crystal. They floated in the air in frozen animation in the foyer. He looked closer and rethought that. No, they weren't frozen still. They moved in a pulsating wave with each breath Jordan took.

She'd saved them. By using her magic, she had assured they wouldn't be cut or worse...

"Jordan..." He didn't want to distract her, but he needed to make sure she was okay. He'd never seen anything like this before. Yeah, when they'd been kids, she'd shown him a few things, but those seemed like parlor tricks compared to this.

"Can't...talk...concentrating..."

He needed to touch her, to help her, so he reached out and held her hips, her body stiffening, and then relaxing in his hold. She smiled and sighed, sending the glass past them, away from the house where it had been thrown after the rock had shattered it, and into the field as it crumbled to dust.

"Holy shit! Did you see that? It was the fucking witch!"

Matt turned and saw the kid with the red hat looking wide-eyed as three of his friends came around a tree, rocks limp in their hands.

Anger poured through him, and he clenched his fists. "What the hell do you think you were doing? You could have killed her!"

"Matt..." Jordan held his wrist, holding him back.

"We didn't do it!" A kid called out.

"We know you threw it," Matt yelled.

"Uh," the little kid blushed and shifted from foot to foot.

The kids blinked, silent, then turned and ran down the street.

"Fuck! I can't believe they threw that shit *knowing* we were standing out here. What if you hadn't been able to control it, Jor? They could have killed you."

She traced a finger down his jaw. "It's okay. We're safe. Let's get out of here."

He closed his eyes and rested his forehead on hers. That had been too close. He just got her back. He didn't want to lose her.

"Oh, I wouldn't be too hasty with that," Prescott said as he meandered his way up the drive, leaving his silver Mercedes running.

They'd been so focused on the kids, they hadn't even noticed Prescott pull up.

"Excuse me?" Matt asked, then clenched his jaw. "What are you doing here?"

Prescott dusted a piece of lint off his tie then raised a brow. "I could ask you the same question. You *are* trespassing on town property after all."

Matt barely resisted the urge to growl. "That means you are doing the same."

"Oh, I don't think so, Mr. Cooper." He sneered the last word, and Matt wanted to punch the man's shiny nose. Ass. "I'm here on official business. As you know, I'm trying to get this monstrosity torn down, and I can't do that if I don't thoroughly inspect the place. And look what you've done. You've broken windows, and who knows what else? I can only blame the mutant behind you for that."

Jordan sucked in a breath, and Matt wanted to carry her home so she didn't have to hear Prescott's vile remarks. But before that, he wanted to cut off the guy's nuts.

"Watch what you say about her, Prescott. Just because you're mayor doesn't give you the right to spout shit."

"Oh, it gives me the perfect right." He quickly dialed his phone and smiled. "Ah, yes, Sheriff? We have a disturbance over at the old Marlow place. I believe some children may be hurt." He smiled and nodded. "Good, I will wait here for you." He pressed end and grinned.

"What the fuck are you talking about? The kids weren't hurt. *They* were the ones who hurt Jordan."

"Oh, really? I don't know. I didn't see that. I came up, and Jordan was using her freak powers to scare poor little children and throw glass at them."

Matt growled and stepped forward.

"Matt, stop. It's not worth it."

"I'm going to kill him."

"Oh, and now I can get you arrested for threatening a public official. Oh, today is turning out to be a good day."

"There they are!" the kid in the red hat said as he pulled his irate parents behind him. "That's the lady that almost killed us with glass."

"Mayor, I'm glad you're here to take care of this problem." The dad, in his too-hot suit leered at Jordan before snarling.

"Don't worry, I'll handle it. She won't be a problem much longer. Ah, here comes the sheriff."

Tyler parked the car and got out, a frown on his face. "What's the problem, Prescott? I don't see any kids hurt. Just Jordan."

Prescott raised his chin and narrowed his eyes. "I want Jordan Cross arrested for endangering children. She almost killed them with glass."

"What the fuck?" Matt yelled. "She didn't touch them. Those kids threw rocks and busted up the windows. Arrest them for vandalism if you're going to arrest anyone."

"I didn't do anything wrong," Jordan whispered, and Matt held her hand, trying to give them both the strength to get through this.

Tyler held up his hands. "Hey now, one thing at a time. Matt, tell me what happened."

Matt opened his mouth to speak, but Prescott cut him off. "I'm the mayor in this town, and you know the laws of Holiday. My word *is* law. I ordered you to arrest the witch; now do it."

The parents nodded their head in agreement, and Tyler's shoulders fell.

"You've got to be fucking kidding me," Matt snarled.

Tyler walked toward them and sighed. "You

know the law, Matt. It's Holiday, not a big city. I'm just a peon in the grand scheme of things. Prescott appointed me because he likes to see the Coopers under his control. I accepted the job so I could help at least somewhat."

"Things need to change," Matt growled.

Tyler glared at him, his color rising. "Then do something about it. Because, as sheriff, I can't. I can only do my best."

"Enough squabbling!" Prescott yelled. "Arrest the witch! Arrest the witch!" The crowd had increased as people came out of their homes, some even joining in with Prescott's chant.

Matt wanted to kill someone. Preferably the mayor from hell. How had he let this happen?

"Matt, it's okay. I'll go with Tyler," Jordan whispered, defeat in her tone. "I don't want to cause any more of a scene."

He turned his back to the crowd and the town he'd called his own. No more. He was done with them. They were cruel to people they didn't understand, and the woman in his arms was more important than anything else in his life.

"Jordan..."

She held her hand up to his lips, silencing him.

"It's not worth it, Matt. Don't get in trouble just by being with me."

"I'm not going to let you go."

"You have to, Matt."

"Guys, I need to take Jordan now," Tyler whispered, his jaw clenched. "I know you didn't do what they say you did, Jor. You're tougher than that."

She looked up at his brother and blinked. "You believe me? But what about…"

"What about what?" Tyler shook his head. "I talked with Abby, I know you're learning control."

"But you still need to arrest her."

Tyler sighed. "Yes, because our town is fucked up, and you can do whatever the fuck you want," he grumbled to Prescott.

Jordan put her hand on Matt's chest and kissed his jaw. "I'll be all right. Go home, Matt."

"I'm going with you."

She shook her head. "No, you're going to go home and work on what we talked about."

"What are you two talking about?" Tyler asked.

"Nothing." Matt scowled. "Fine, but come to

me when you're out."

She nodded, her shoulders straight.

"I'll take care of her, brother."

"You better," he growled.

"What's taking so long?" Prescott whined. "Cuff her."

Tyler shook his head. "No, she's coming willingly. I don't need to cuff her."

Prescott's face grew red. "She's a danger to society. I said cuff her."

"No, I won't do that. It's in my rights as sheriff to at least decide whether or not to cuff someone."

Prescott huffed. "Well, we'll just see about that."

Tyler put Jordan in the back of the cruiser and closed the door softly. He got in the front, and Matt watched as his brother drove the love of his life to jail.

Fuck this shit. There needed to be some changes in this town. The days of Prescott's reign of terror were numbered.

"Remember whose side you're on, Cooper," Prescott taunted. "Because when the shit hits the fan, you don't want to cross me."

Matt narrowed his eyes. "Oh, I'll remember which side I'm on." He pushed past the crowd, using a little more force than necessary, and walked to his home.

He had a lot to think about, but first, he needed to breathe because he was about to kill someone and he didn't need to be arrested by his brother. There had been enough of that already.

Chapter 10

The hammer caught the edge of his thumb, and Matt cursed. Well, that seemed about right for the kind of day he was having. He paused, no, not the whole day. The early morning when he'd been buried in Jordan had been fucking spectacular. It had just happened to go downhill after that.

After he got home, he'd showered, ate a quick bite, and then he drove over to Jackson's to use his garage. He wasn't in the mood to work today and had called in. Sally had been surprised, but she didn't ask any questions. Even though he'd moved out ages ago, he still liked to work with his hands and create things in the place where he'd worked as a kid. Even though he'd tried to tire himself, so he wouldn't think about his problems, they still bugged him.

He hated this town. He'd never thought he'd have to say that, but he did. He'd grown up here and never thought he'd want to leave. But the way the citizens had treated Jordan today...

He put the hammer aside and picked up a piece of sandpaper. With each stroke, his anger built. They'd rallied against her. Not all of them, but enough that he wanted to vomit. He didn't know how he was going to do it, but he was going to change the minds of Holiday. They weren't some backwoods, inbred town. No, they were a nice group of people who didn't know about magic so they acted out of fear.

Something they would have to pay for.

They also were being led by a sadistic bastard who had it out for Jordan. Prescott St. James needed to be put out of Matt's misery. The rules set in place by their ancestors were outdated and just plain wrong. That Prescott could have whomever he wanted arrested was a farce and mockery of the law. No wonder Tyler hated his job.

Matt sanded down a corner of the box and sighed. He had no idea how he was going to do it. He sure as hell didn't want to be mayor. No one really did, and that was the problem. Nobody wanted the job, and those who might want it didn't want to deal with Prescott. It was clear something had to change because they couldn't go on living like this.

He stood back and looked at the half-finished box. When it was finished, it would be an herb box for Jordan. She had the garden in the back of her grandmother's place, but she didn't have anything for just herself. Something he wanted to change, even if it was just a pipe dream since she was leaving. Maybe if she saw this, she'd see the possibility of roots and proof he wanted her to stay.

He just had to make sure it was *worth* staying. Because, at the moment, he knew Jordan didn't want to stay. It wasn't safe, not with Prescott in charge and the town rallying against her. There were some folks who hadn't reacted that way, but they hadn't stood up for her either.

That would have to change.

He took out a drawer and sanded the sides. When it was finished, it would house her herbs. They could grow on top and be store, dried, in the drawers. Tyler had told him she was practicing with her magic more so he wanted to help. Though he still felt hesitant about the whole magic thing, he had to get over it. He'd been wrong. Jordan would never knowingly have hurt him. And if she learned more about her powers, she could help both herself and him.

Hopefully.

"So let me get this straight," Justin said as he leaned against the workbench. "You just let her go to jail and left her there?"

Matt scowled and shook his head. "Tyler and Jordan told me not to go. That it would only make things worse. So now I'm stuck here while Jordan is alone in a cell and Prescott is grinning like the ass he is."

Justin sighed. "I can't believe Tyler actually did it."

"He didn't have a choice."

"Really? Because it isn't like he's the law or anything."

Matt ground his teeth together. "Not in this town. He's just a fucking glorified figurehead."

Justin cursed and handed Matt a level. "That needs to change."

"You think?"

"So, what are we going to do?"

"That's the thing. Other than getting Prescott out of office, I don't see much we *can* do. But who would run against him?"

Justin visibly shuddered. "Not me, that's for sure. I barely have enough time with being principal as it is. And I think it says something in the bylaws that I can't do it anyway since it would be a conflict of interest."

Matt raised a brow. "Really?"

Justin smiled, showing teeth. "Yep. But you know, you could do it. You're a business owner and a good seed in society and all that shit."

"Lovely," he said dryly.

"What? It's the truth."

Yeah, but could he really be mayor and be forever linked to the old Marlow place? He couldn't quite see himself ducking out of an event because he had to turn all ghosty.

"Maybe Jackson?"

Justin smiled with unholy glee at Matt's suggestion, and they both broke out laughing.

"Oh God, please, please can I be the one to ask?" Justin asked, rubbing his hands together.

"I can just imagine his face when he tells you no."

"Oh, you mean the *I'm-a-badass-with-coal-and-ice-for-a-heart* face? The one he gives us when we ask if we can decorate his house with garland and pictures of hot girls dressed as sexy elves for Christmas?"

"You know, I think that was one of your more enlightened ideas, bro."

"What? Come one, we're five single guys. We should be allowed to put up pictures of scantily clad women on our walls as decoration if we want to."

"Really? So this is what men talk about when the women are behind bars?" Jordan teased as she walked into the garage. She looked pale, shaky, and in need of a hug. But she was here.

Thank God.

Matt quickly, and discreetly, pushed the herb box to the side of the room behind a bench so she couldn't see it and walked to her. He opened his arms, and she sank in his hold, her body pressed tightly against his.

"I missed you," she whispered.

"I missed you too, baby." He kissed the top of her head and ran a hand down her back.

"Sure," she said with a dry twist. "So much so that you're talking about naked elves. Hot."

"Actually, Justin was the one who mentioned it."

"Thanks for throwing me under the bus, bro," Justin said. "Come here, Jor. Let me get a good look at you." He held open his arms, and

Jordan extricated herself from Matt's and walked to his brother.

Matt raised a brow. "Watch your hands, Justin."

"Sure, I'll watch them as they rub—*Oof.*" Justin rubbed his side where Jordan had elbowed him. "'K, that hurt."

"Keep your hands where I can see them— *not* on me. And aren't you the principal of the school? I thought you'd reformed your bad boy ways."

"Obviously not enough." Justin gave a wicked smile and winked.

Jordan shook her head but smiled. "I swear you Cooper brothers are in a league of your own."

"As long as you know there's no crying in baseball," Justin joked.

Matt groaned. "Oh God, I think that was the worst joke you've ever told."

Justin smiled. "Actually, no. Remember the one where—"

Jordan smiled and placed her hand over his mouth. "I think I'm good without knowing whatever you're about to say."

Matt growled. "Jor, could you refrain from

touching my brother's lips?"

Justin nipped at them, and Jordan took her hand back. "You're horrible, Justin."

"True," Justin agreed. "So, how was the slammer?"

"I would think you'd know, dear troublemaker."

Justin raised his hands in mock innocence. "Hey, I never got caught. There's a difference."

Matt shook his head. "As much as I love you, Justin, go."

Jordan gasped. "Hey, rude."

"Actually, I have to go help Abby with some last minute things for the play tonight. I would say you should come, but with what happened today, I don't know if you'd want to make a scene."

Jordan shook her head. "I know. I just want to stay home."

"You'll stay with me," Matt growled.

"Oh, really?" Jordan raised a brow.

"Oh, look, a lovers' quarrel. I should go." Justin tugged Jordan close and hugged her tight. "I'm glad you're okay, hon," he said seriously. "We'll fix this."

Jordan shook her head and kissed his cheek. "I don't think this can be fixed."

"You obviously don't realize your boyfriend over there is a fixer. We Coopers stand together, and you're an honorary one, babe."

Jordan teared up, and Matt held her close to him. God, he loved his family. They were accepting of anyone who they considered family. Maybe they wouldn't freak out as much when, and if, he told them he was a ghost...then again, maybe not.

"You two stand together, and you'll be fine." Justin smiled, a little sadness in his gaze before he masked it, and then he walked out of the garage.

Matt kissed her neck, and she moaned. He pulled back but kept that thought for later. "Are you sure you're okay?"

Jordan turned in his arms and looked up at him. "I'm a bit jarred, but okay. Tyler didn't put me in a cell."

Matt closed his eyes and let out a sigh of relief. "That's good."

"He just made me sit there for a couple of hours with breakfast and hide out from Prescott."

"I'm going to kill that man."

"Who? Tyler?" She tried to smile, but it fell flat.

Matt pulled her into his arms and kissed her neck. The shiver that slid down her body made him think of naughty things. Naughty things that they could be doing right now if they wanted. First, he needed to make her feel better.

"I'm going to figure out a way to get Prescott out of office since I don't want my brother arresting me for murder."

Jordan looked up at him, her eyes tired and weary. "I don't want you getting hurt or losing your job, Matt."

"I'm not letting you be the catalyst for Prescott's hatred."

She shook her head then rested it on his chest. "It's nothing that I didn't get used to when I lived here before."

A sharp pang speared him. How could he have let her feel this way in the town where they'd both grown up? It was no wonder she'd left. He tightened his grip, and she snuggled closer.

"Are you hungry?" She'd been gone for over two hours, and though she'd said Tyler had fed her, he still wanted to take care of her.

"No, I don't think I could eat anything."

He ran a hand through her hair then kissed the top of her head. "Let's head over to my place and be lazy. What do you say?"

Jordan kissed the bottom of his jaw and nodded. "That sounds perfect. But I still have a lot to do on the house."

He tried not to think of the fact that she as getting closer and closer to leaving him. Maybe a distraction would work.

He kissed her softly, letting his tongue run along the seam of her mouth. She moaned into his mouth, and he ran a hand down her back, cupping her ass. She wiggled into him and let out a laugh.

"Hey, I'm putting on my best moves here, why are you laughing?" He squeezed her ass, and she laughed hard.

"I'm sorry, baby. I love how you distract me."

"Uh-huh. Then why are you laughing?"

"Because we're in Jackson's garage."

Matt looked around at their surroundings and frowned. "I don't understand. We could make love here. I could bend you over that work bench." If fact, that sounded like a fucking fantastic idea.

She shook her head, but her eyes had darkened at the suggestion. "Take me to your place, and you can bend me over something there." She grinned, and he groaned. Her hand crept down his stomach and brushed against his cock, which was currently trying to escape his jeans.

"Is your car still at the old Marlow place?" God, it was getting too hard to think about logistics. They needed to get to his place—now.

"Yep, that means you need to drive with a hard-on and not crash."

He groaned and kissed her hard, her tongue fighting with his. He pulled back, panting. "Get in the car."

She grinned and lowered her eyes. "Race you."

"Baby, I'm about to make it to the finish line right now if you don't hurry up that ass of yours."

She huffed, but her eyes held laughter. With a wink, she ran out the garage toward the car. He closed his eyes, took a deep breath, and willed his cock to calm down.

"Come on, buddy, just hold on until we get there. The last thing we need do is crash because you're too busy thinking about Jordan."

"Are you talking to your dick?" Jordan asked as she walked back in.

Matt growled. "Get in the car." He felt his cheeks heat up. Yeah, she wasn't supposed to have heard that little pep talk of his.

Jordan laughed—God, he loved that sound—and he ran behind her.

Somehow, they got to his place and stood in his living room, panting, needy, and staring at each other.

"So, does he talk back?" Jordan asked, a small smile on her face.

"Why don't you come over and see?"

They broke out into laughter. "Oh God, that has to be the worst line ever."

Matt shrugged. "Hey, you're the one asking if my dick talks."

She shook her head, and he smiled. "Did you say something about bending me over something here?"

Matt's cock rose—again, damn thing—and he groaned. He prowled toward her, determination in his stride. Her breath hitched, and he crushed his mouth to hers, wrapping her ponytail around his fist. He trailed his other hand up her shirt and cupped her breast.

She wiggled, and he pinched her nipple and rolled it.

"Matt, God, that feels good."

"Good? Oh, I think I can do better."

He pulled her backward and brought them to his kitchen table.

"What is it with you and tables?" she asked as she kissed his neck.

"I can't help it. I see one, and I want to fuck you over it." He tugged off her shirt and groaned when her braless tits bounced.

"That could prove disastrous in public." She moaned, and he sucked a nipple into his mouth

"True," he mumbled around her breast. He pulled back and rubbed her pussy through her jeans. Fuck, she was hot, ready. "Maybe we should fuck it out of our systems. You know, just to be sure."

"I like that idea. But, first, I want to do something for you."

He raised an eyebrow as she took off his shirt. "Oh, really?"

"Uh-huh." She knelt before him and undid his jeans. She lowered them past his ass then off completely. He sidestepped them so he only stood in his boxer briefs.

"Jordan, you don't have to—" *Fuck*. She'd pulled him out of his boxers and stroked him. She raised her head so she gazed directly at him as she licked the head.

Holy. Shit.

She lowered her gaze and licked the vein

underneath. His body rocked as pleasure shot through him. He held onto the table with one hand and her ponytail with the other so he wouldn't fall.

She looked up at him again and swallowed him whole. He groaned as she relaxed her throat muscles and took him deeper. He forced himself not to thrust even though his balls ached. As if sensing that, she reached up and rolled them in her hand.

"Jesus, Jor," he let out, his voice raspy.

She hummed, the vibrations shooting through his cock and up his spine. He went cross-eyed as she took her hand and stroked him in rhythm with her other movements.

"Baby, I'm not going to last."

She hummed again and continued her delicious torture. He pulled back, and she pouted.

"Hey, I wasn't done."

"No, but I would be if you didn't stop."

"So? I wanted a taste."

He groaned and tried to not to come. Jordan would be the death of him. "I'm not that young anymore, baby. I might not have quite the recovery time to make love to you after that."

She pouted but didn't look all too sad. He

bent, gripped her hips, and pulled her to a standing position. She gasped as he took off her pants and panties in a quick movement.

"You're getting good at that," she teased.

"You'll just have to let me practice."

She rolled her eyes. "I swear your lines are getting worse."

He spanked her, and she gasped. "Watch it, babe. I may just have to show you who's boss."

She narrowed her eyes. "Oh, then you'll find out that would be me."

Matt grinned. "True, but when I'm fucking you, you'll have a clearer picture."

"Uh-huh."

He gripped her hips and turned her around. She gasped and gripped the edge of the table.

"Matt..."

"Shh, baby, I'll take care of you." He knelt behind her, and she wiggled. He gave her a sharp slap on her other cheek, and she moaned. "See? You like that?" His cock hit his stomach and throbbed, but he wanted to look his fill before he filled her.

He placed both hands on her now rosy ass and massaged. She groaned and bent farther down on the table so her delicious ass was now closer to his face. Taking that as a hint, he nibbled, licked, and bit down.

"Matt!"

He licked the spot where he'd bit and spread her cheeks. He lowered his head and kissed her pussy. She squirmed, and he smiled. He licked and sucked her clit while forcing her legs to spread wider so he could get a better taste. Fuck, she tasted amazing—sweet, ripe, Jordan. He licked again, this time spearing her with his tongue. She shook and called out, but he didn't stop. Magic sparked around him, engulfing the room in a soft glow. He nibbled around her clit before licking her again, and her pussy clenched around his tongue as she screamed his name. He licked farther up until he reached her little star-shaped hole and sucked around it.

"Matt? What are you doing?" she said breathless.

"Mmm, just tasting." He gently dipped his tongue inside. She froze then moaned. He repeated the process a few times, her body shaking, his along with hers.

"Matt, please, I need you."

He moved his hands so they gripped her hips and he stood behind her. "God, I need you too."

"Maybe one day, we can try..." Her whole body blushed, and he almost came on her back.

"Dear God, yes."

She let out a raspy chuckle, her breasts resting on the table. Yeah, he wouldn't eat there again and not think about the best thing he'd ever tasted. He positioned his cock at her entrance and stood still, the tip barely brushing her wet folds. He gulped, fighting for control. He didn't want to come as soon as her pussy was wrapped around him.

She rotated her hips, her ass in the air, ready. He slowly entered her, her pussy tightening as he pushed in inch by inch. She groaned, and he echoed her. When he was fully seated within her, his balls and thighs against her, he bent over her back and kissed her nape.

"I love you," he whispered, unable to hold it in any longer.

Tears fell down her cheeks. And she swallowed hard. He froze. What if she didn't feel the same way? Here he was, deep inside her, professing his love, and she didn't speak.

"I love you too, Matt."

He let out a breath, kissed her cheek, and closed his eyes. He pulled out partially and then slid back in. She moaned, and he did it again, this time faster...harder. He stood up, gripped her hips, and slammed into her.

"Matt!"

God, he loved his name on her lips. He pistoned into her, her pussy clenching around him as his balls tightened. Again, little sparks of magic flew into the air, filling the space with warmth. He felt her come right before he couldn't hold back anymore, and he released inside of her. His dick twitched and throbbed, his seed warm inside her and around him. He lowered his body over hers, careful not to let too much of his weight lay on top of her.

"Did you mean it?" she finally whispered after a few minutes of blessed silence.

"That I love you?" He pulled out of her, his cock finally softening, and turned her around so he could look in her eyes. "Of course I meant it. I love you, Jor. I always have."

She nodded, tears running down her cheeks. "Good, because I meant it, too."

Chapter 11

Jordan couldn't believe Halloween was already here. Or rather, for her, All Hallows Eve. As a witch, she should have loved the holiday. It should have been a time where she could embrace what she was and could be caught up in the magic of it all.

But, in reality, it reminded her of what people thought of her and their attitudes. They dressed up as hags, and called themselves witches, and threw things at her.

Jordan didn't want any of that. She'd rather be at home practicing her magic or just cuddling with Matt.

She fixed the pointy hat on top of her head and grinned. With the black dress and hat, she looked like the very best commercial witch. If she couldn't beat them, she'd join them. No matter how much she tried helping after school or during the art program, she still hadn't won over the town. She hated the way people treated her—and continued to treat her, but at least she was taking proactive steps to change it.

Tonight, she'd be going with Abby to the children's' Halloween play. Abby had put her whole heart into the event and Jordan would be by her side to make sure everything went off without a hitch. There was still some tension between her friend and Tyler, but Abby was smiling through it, and so would Jordan.

When she'd first come to town, it had been to find herself and clean her grandmother's house. Yet, as she started to make friends with Abby and Ali, and then the Coopers, she found herself thinking of making Holiday her home again. Could she do it? Ignore the looks and whispers?

Well, she loved Matt, so she would have to.

She wanted him therefore she needed to get over herself and stay.

She could do it.

She had to.

That meant she needed to get the town on her side. Easier said than done, but she could it. All she had to do was laugh at herself and show she could be a contributor to the community. Though she didn't have a job, she could at least volunteer until she found something she loved. She couldn't be a PR rep anymore, not in this little town. The only job that could use her experience was that of the Mayor and there was no way she would do that.

Not with Prescott running things and scaring the town.

Jordan stood in her house—no, her grandmother's house. She had to stop thinking about it as hers. Because the more she did, the harder it would be to leave. She already felt a pull with the place, and it freaked her out. She could already feel the place calling her home. The same way she didn't want to feel at home in Matt's arms.

She took a shuddering breath. It hurt to think that Matt could already be dead... No, that wasn't the case. He was just a part-time spirit. It was odd as hell, almost as if someone had put a spell on him or dosed him with a potion.

By whom or how they'd done it... she didn't know. When she wasn't cleaning and polishing the house, she was looking up what she could do to fix things. She had a few ideas, but short of going balls-to-the-wall and praying something worked by just experimenting she didn't know what to do.

"Jordan? You in here?" Matt's voice echoed down the hallway, and surprised to find tears on her cheeks, she quickly wiped them away.

"I'm here." Thankfully, her voice didn't betray her emotional turmoil, and she walked out of the office and into the living room where Matt stood with a broom in his hand.

Darn it. He still looked sexy.

Why she thought he'd changed in the two hours since she'd seen him was beyond her guess.

Her face brightened up, and a little part of her melted. The traitorous part. She finally looked at him and laughed.

"A flying monkey, really?" He had on fake wings, a partial monkey suit, big ears, and a cute little red top hat.

He shrugged, forcing his wings to bob up and down with him. "Hey, you're my witch, so I'm your monkey."

"But I'm not green this time."

"Good, because now I can taste your skin and not the paint."

She blushed and laughed. "You ready to get this kiddie play over with?"

He pulled her into his arms and smiled. "I thought you were excited about it."

Tension crept through her shoulders. "Oh, I am. Just worried as well."

He frowned and kissed her temple. "I'll take care of you."

"You don't need to. I need to take care of myself." She had to.

"Then I'll be by your side."

She smiled again and they left to go to the play. When they got there, Matt left to go see Tyler and Jordan looked for her friend. Abby was running around in her Little Bo Peep costume, herding the children in their costumes as if they were her sheep.

"Abby," Jordan called out. "Can I help?"

Her friend gave her a bright smile and sighed. "Yes, thank God you're here. Can you help Tim and Samantha? They each have little tears in their costumes and I don't have time to sew them up."

Jordan nodded and walked toward the little kids. Both had tear-stained cheeks and wide eyes.

"Hey, guys. Let me help, okay?"

Tim nodded, dressed in his in vampire costume, his little fake fangs sticking out of his mouth.

"Here's the sewing kit," Samantha said as she handed Jordan a small box. She was dressed like a little princess, complete with a sparkly tiara. "Ms. Brewer said she'd back soon, but she's all alone." Her little lip quivered and Jordan wanted to hug these two close.

"It's okay, you guys. I can handle a couple of ripped seams." They both nodded and Jordan set to work, loving the way she felt needed. Once she was done, they both gave her hugs and Jordan held back tears.

With the kids on their way, Jordan left the backstage area to find Matt and froze.

"Come on, Matt, dump that little witch and get your head on straight," Stacey whined as she pressed her perky breasts into his arm. She was dressed as a naughty nurse and Jordan wanted to vomit.

He didn't move back.

Jordan blinked, trying to tone down the hurt crawling through her. Matt hadn't noticed she'd come in.

"You know you wanted to go to the Halloween party with me, Mattie. It will be a great way to get ready for our wedding." Stacey fluttered her eyelashes, shimmied against him, then leaned forward and brushed her lips against his.

There wasn't a hole close enough for Jordan to crawl into and die.

Matt didn't move.

Rage tore through her, and she forced herself not to use her magic. This time, unlike with Abby, she controlled her magic and didn't harm Stacey, though she wanted to. The magic scraped at her skin, wanting to burst out, but cooled when Jordan focused.

Matt finally pushed Stacey off, and Jordan wanted to vomit. Really, Matt? Like five minutes after they'd left each other happy, he kisses another woman? Okay, he was the one who had been kissed, but he took a hell of a long time pushing her off him.

"Stacey, stop," Matt grumbled, and wiped his mouth with his forearm. *Score.*

"What? Why can't we profess our love?" Stacey whined.

"Jesus, Stacey. I don't understand you. We're not together. We've never been together. We're not ever going to be together. So, stop rubbing yourself on me and creating a scene. You're only embarrassing yourself."

Stacey paled then straightened her shoulders. She snarled and pasted a look of revenge on her face. "We'll see, Matt. We'll see." She stormed out, and Matt finally looked up to see Jordan.

"Jordan."

She stared into his eyes and squared her shoulders, ready to get whatever was going to happen over with as quickly as possible. "Can we talk, Matt?"

Jordan looked around at the people staring and whispering. Great, she was the center of attention again.

He nodded, a frown on his face. The play had started, so they crept out the side door, not wanting to interrupt more than they already had. She followed him, and he shut the door behind them.

"How the hell could you let Stacey kiss you?"

Matt's face reddened, whether from anger or embarrassment she didn't know. She was too pissed off to care.

"Well?"

"I can't hit a woman. You know that."

Jordan growled. "So you just stand there and let her lay her pressed-on nails on you?"

"Jealous?" The bastard grinned.

"Fuck you, Matt. She *kissed* you and let her perky tits touch you. I hated it. And you just *stood* there!"

"She surprised me with the kiss. As for the pressing of body parts, it was either stand there or choke her to death. I don't want to go to prison."

"Then learn the fucking two-step and dance away."

Matt smiled. "Aww, baby, you care."

"Of course I fucking care. I love you, you bastard."

He threw back his head and laughed. "God, I love you."

"You better." She cracked a smile, and he kissed her softly, his lips tasting of the coffee he'd drunk that morning.

"I'm sorry I freaked out."

Matt sighed and pulled them to a chair. He sat down, and she got on his lap, ignoring his erection.

"Tell me why you left all those years ago, Jordan."

She froze. That hadn't been what she'd

expected.

"You know why," she said evenly. "I couldn't take it anymore."

He shook his head. "I know that, but something had to have triggered it. Tell me."

She sat on his lap, her back ramrod straight, and her lungs feeling like they would collapse. Could she tell him? After all these years, she didn't know if she could voice the words caught on her tongue like a heavy film.

"I left because I didn't feel safe."

"What happened, Jor?" He rubbed his hand down her spine, and she leaned against him, taking in the comfort he offered.

She took a deep breath. "The night that I was supposed to meet you for our date, Prescott stopped me."

Matt's hold tightened, but he didn't say anything.

"He told me he'd wanted me from the start, and he..." Her voice caught, and she bit her lip so she wouldn't vomit.

"Did he touch you?" Matt growled, a promise of death on his tone.

"He tried... He got real close. He had my

pants around my ankles before I could fight him off."

Matt cursed and hugged her tighter. "I'm going to kill him."

"I stopped him, Matt. But I had to use magic to do it. I didn't hurt him, not really, but I stunned him. If I had listened to my grandmother and actually trained, it wouldn't have gotten as far as it had."

"Oh, baby." He cupped her face and kissed her. She let him comfort her, though inside she wanted to shrivel up and die. No matter how hard she tried to be strong, the feel of Prescott's hands on her would never go away. It was as if he'd imprinted on her. No amount of bleach or soap would wash it away.

"I hurt him, Matt. At least I stunned him."

"Good."

"No, it's not good. Magic isn't supposed to hurt. It's supposed to be good. And I used it to harm him."

"You did it to protect yourself."

She shook her head. "That doesn't make it right."

"You didn't have a choice, Jor. It's not your fault."

"I don't know why he isn't scared of me. I would be."

"Baby, he probably is, that's why he's an ass. But you're not to blame."

"But Prescott blamed me for leading him on. He told me I'd hexed him, at least that's what he says. I didn't hex him, but he took my small burst of magic and made sure I knew he could hurt me with his words and threats. He said he'd hurt you and your bothers and find a way to make you guys pay for my mistake."

Matt cursed. "So you left to protect us?"

"I left because I needed to. Yes, to protect you. And myself."

"Jordan Cross. I love you. I loved you then, and I love you even more now. You don't get to decide how to protect me as much as I don't get to decide for you. We're a team. We need to decide together."

"I don't know how to fix it. But I'm not sorry I did it. I mean, I'm not sorry I saved myself. I had to, Matt. Thank you for saying that. It wasn't my fault."

"That's why we need to work together. We'll figure out how to fix my problem and take care of Prescott."

"You make it sound easy. Just talking about

it doesn't help anything."

"But not talking about things just buries them and makes it worse."

She smiled and kissed his cheek. "Look at you wanting to talk about your feelings."

He smiled wryly. "Just don't tell my brothers."

"I'll keep your sensitive side a secret. Just make sure you take care of yourself as good as you're trying to take care of me."

He kissed her, promises of hope and a future in his hold. "I promise."

Jordan just hoped she could rely on that. Because if she lost him because of who she was, she might not be able to live with herself, nor would she want to.

Chapter 12

Matt tugged Jordan closer as they walked down the path to the old Marlow place after the play ended. The sun would be setting in about twenty minutes, and they wanted to be securely inside before that happened. Kids started to come out of their homes, dressed as superheroes and princesses, ready to start trick-or-treating.

A full moon on Halloween.

Just what a ghost like him needed.

He hated when the two of them fell on the same day because, more often than not, a group of kids would gain some courage and find a way to break in. Then Matt would have to hide. On occasion, he'd make a noise and try to spook them away.

As long as people thought the place was haunted, they usually left him alone.

Until Prescott had decided to be an ass about it and decided he wanted to tear the house down.

His jaw clenched at the thought of the rat bastard. He'd tried to rape Jordan, and Matt was going to kill him.

Slowly.

"Stop growling. You're scaring the children." Jordan elbowed his side, and he kissed the top of her head.

"It's Halloween. They're supposed to be scared."

"Yeah, but not by a guy walking around in plain clothes."

"Serves them right." He grinned, and she just shook her head.

"You're impossible."

"Yeah, but you still love me."

"I have no idea why."

"I think it has something to do with tables."

She blushed and looked around, though no one was paying them any attention. "Matt..."

"What can I say? I'll never be able to sit down and think about dinner the same way again."

"I swear I can't take you anywhere."

"And yet, all I want to do is take you."

She rolled her eyes as they walked inside. "All you think about is sex."

"Not true. I also think about sports, ghosts, witches, and whether or not Montana will ever have a pro-baseball team. But yes, sex is about ninety percent of my overall thinking."

"Only ninety?"

"Some days are tougher than others." He pulled her close, loving the feel of her in his arms.

"Yeah, sure." She pulled his head down, and their lips met. Gods, he loved the taste of her, like sweet berries and lilac.

He deepened the kiss, their bodies entwining as he lifted her off the floor so she could wrap her legs around his waist. He kneaded her ass as he walked to the wall. She arched against him, her core rubbing his cock through their jeans.

He pulled back and rested his forehead on hers. "We need to stop. The sun is about to go down, and I don't want to drop you. Plus, I don't think we want to try and make love when I'm a ghost. That might be a little too weird."

She smiled and kissed his brow while lowering her legs. "We could always try it."

He laughed. "That's why I love you."

"Because, apparently, I have an odd kink?"

"Of course." A sharp pang shot through him, and he bent over.

"Matt?"

He let out a breath. "It's okay; I'm just changing."

"You never told me it would hurt *this* much." She knelt before him and rubbed his arms.

Pain rocketed through him, and he closed his eyes. He felt his body grow heavy then light as a feather. He could feel Jordan's hand on his arm, centering him. Then gradually, her touch faded. He felt his body shift, and he floated toward that cool almost nothingness that had stalked him for all these years.

He opened his eyes and met Jordan's gaze to see tears running down her cheeks.

"We'll fix this, Matt."

"I know, baby." He was just humoring her. He didn't believe it for one second. He'd been like this for eleven years, and he didn't think that would change.

"You're so cold," she whispered. "At least the air around you since I can't actually feel you. I don't think I'll ever get used to it."

He smiled wryly. "I don't want you to have to."

"So, what would you like to do this Halloween? Scare children?"

He laughed, letting her change the subject. "Not tonight. Let another haunted house do the scaring."

Her eyes brightened. "Really? There's another haunted house in Holiday?"

He let out a breath. "You're lucky you're pretty."

She growled. "You're lucky I can't touch you, or I'd kick you in the nuts for that."

"Wanna play chess?"

Jordan sighed. "Fine, but don't think you're off the hook."

"Oh, I wouldn't expect you to ever let me off the hook."

They played a few games as the night wore on and the sounds of children quieted as they went home for the night. He beat her a few times, but she got better as they practiced.

Jordan paused while she was about to take his queen and looked around. "Do you smell smoke?"

Matt froze, focusing so he could use his senses. He could easily see and hear, but tasting and smell took a bit longer. The acrid smell of smoke burned his cool nostrils. He could hear the crackling of sparks as the flames grew near, though he couldn't see them.

"Fuck, I think there's a fire. We need to get out of here."

Jordan looked at him, fear in her gaze.

"I know, baby."

"But, Matt, you can't leave. If the place burns..."

She didn't finish, but he knew what she was going to say. If the place burned to the ground, he'd be lost forever.

"I have to get you out of here."

"Not without you," Jordan said, her tone filled with determination, though her voice quavered with fear.

"Please, Jordan." He felt the door and coolness greeted his touch, and he cursed. He didn't know whether it was from himself or the door.

Jordan followed his movements and did the same with her hand. "It's not warm. We have time. Let me try to put out the fire with my magic. I'm not losing you, Matt."

He wanted to kiss her, hold her, and get her the fuck out of the house. But all he could do was watch as she opened the door and walked out into the hallway. He cursed but followed her. A flicking light met him, but the bright yellow and orange glow warmed his cool body and scared the shit out of him.

Fuck. It didn't look like they had a way out.

Smoke filled the room and the roar of the flames grew louder as the fire heightened, the flames licking the air and scorching the walls. Dust and particles fell from celling and lit up as they touched the flames. He looked up and would have paled if he were able to. The ceiling looked like it was going to go at any moment.

The old Marlow house had no hope. It would burn to the ground, and his tie to this world would be lost forever. He took a deep breath and fisted his hands. He had to get Jordan out. He might not be long for this world, but he wouldn't let Jordan die for him.

"Jordan, we need to get you out. Now!" he yelled over the roar of the fire.

"Not without you," she choked out as the smoke increased. She held up her hands, magic pouring out of her. The sparks and little balls of light flitted around her and formed a bright glow. Shockingly, he could feel the warmth.

Jordan flexed her hands and he watched her eyes narrow. The magic engulfed the sparks and edges of the bright orange flames. As the magic ebbed, the flames lowered slightly and pulled back. The flames would fight and Jordan would groan, shooting out more power.

"Stop being stubborn!" It didn't matter if she stopped the fire now. It was too late for the house.

"It's working, Matt. I can stop this." She narrowed her gaze and focused on the fire. He could feel her magic like a static energy on his ghostly arms. She funneled her strength, and he held his breath.

"Jordan. Even if you do this, you need to go."

"Matt, I can do this. I'm not leaving you. I

love you."

"I love you too, but—" The sound of Jordan's scream cut him off.

Matt watched in horror as a fallen ceiling timber knocked her down and she crumbed to the ground, unconscious. He ran to her side and watched as her chest rose and fell.

Thank God she was breathing.

He pulled at the hunk of wood and cursed. It was too heavy for him. Fuck this. He needed to get Jordan the hell out of there. He took a deep breath, grabbed the timber with both hands and yanked. Somehow, it lifted off her, and he threw it to the side. He knelt beside her and tried not to freak out.

He couldn't touch her.

She wasn't part of the house.

The flames moved closer without Jordan's magic, and he cursed.

"Jordan! Wake up!"

She didn't move.

He screamed in frustration. "Are you fucking kidding me? All of this and I'm going to lose her because I can't fucking touch her? She's my everything, and you're going to let her die because

I'm a fucking *ghost*? Some fate I got in life, huh? This fucking sucks. Someone help me!"

Ghostly tears ran down his pale cheeks, and he reached, unconsciously, to trace her cheek. Her skin felt warm to his touch.

Wait. He'd felt her skin?

Matt put his hand on her shoulder and squeezed. Fuck. He could touch her. He didn't know what had happened. Maybe fate, someone, anyone, had finally listened to him, but he didn't care. He took her in his arms and stood. The flames were approaching, but he could see a path to the front door.

He took a deep breath and closed his eyes. Once he crossed the threshold, he'd be gone. No more Matt Cooper. Once the fire ate its way through the house, there wouldn't be anything left to tether anyway.

He kissed Jordan's forehead and took a step toward the door.

"I love you, baby."

He held her close, keeping the heat away from her, and walked through the charred and burned door. Wood splintered around them, sparking in the flames as it licked around him. He stared at the shocked expressions on his brothers' faces and grunted. They must have shown up when they'd seen the flames, but Matt couldn't focus on them.

He laid Jordan on the ground beside the porch, traced her brow with his fingers, and felt himself fading away.

He heard his brothers' screams as he tugged and lashed out at the hands trying to carry him to away to the place he had disappeared to before. Tendrils of panic tore at him as he fought their control.

Matt didn't want to die. He wanted a future with Jordan. He fought, tearing the hands from his body. It felt like he was underwater, the pressure intense as he tried to surface. He focused on Jordan's face...on the future he wanted to have. With a kick and a twist, he took a gasping breath and looked down at his solid arms.

Solid.

Fuck.

"Matt!" Jordan threw herself into his arms, tears running down her face.

"Jordan?"

"Oh, God. How did you do it? You're real, baby. Oh, my God. Is it over?"

He wrapped his arms around her, inhaled her smoky lilac scent, and choked out a sob.

"I think they let me go."

"They? Matt, we didn't see anything. We just saw you fighting and fading away."

"I don't know, baby."

"What the fuck was that, Matt?" Jackson asked as he stormed over. He pulled Matt out of Jordan's hold and held him tightly. "Don't ever scare us like that again."

Justin wrapped an arm around Jordan's shoulders and kissed her cheek. Matt didn't feel jealous. He was too relieved to feel much of anything else. Brayden cursed under his breath and slapped a soot-covered hand on his back.

"So, you're a ghost?"

Matt gulped. "Uh, I was."

"And you never bothered to mention it?" Jackson asked, his gaze stormy.

"I didn't want to bother y'all."

"Fuck that shit." Justin scowled. "We're Coopers. No secrets."

"Next time I'll tell you."

"There better not be a next time, Matt," Jordan warned.

"Okay, baby, anything you want."

"Get you're filthy hands off me!" Stacey screamed, and Tyler pulled her out from behind a bush. "My brother will have your badge for this."

The sheriff shook his head. "Oh, I don't think so, hon. You were standing by with matches and gas cans, and reek of the shit."

"Language!"

"You have worse problems then my language, kid."

"Get your hands off my sister!" Prescott screamed, and shoved through the crowd that Matt had just noticed.

Well, so much for his secret.

"Not this time, Prescott," Tyler warned.

"I'm the mayor! You have to listen to me."

"Not when you have soot on your pants."

Prescott paled. "I'm...I'm surrounded by fire. What do you expect?"

"You wouldn't have it on your pants if you were just coming on to the scene. You're an idiot."

"I demand you stop these vile lies! I'm the mayor!" Even as he said it, he started backing up. The crowed didn't part for him this time.

Good for them.

"You know, I think it's high passed time we change that," Jackson drawled, a scowl on face.

"No one will run against me."

"Oh, shut your capped mouth," Jackson shouted.

"My teeth are not fake!"

"I capped them myself, you bastard," Jackson said, frowning.

The crowd broke out in laughter, and Matt shook his head. These people needed to learn to stand up for themselves and not do what Prescott demanded of them. Maybe tonight would help.

"Prescott, you're done!" Matt yelled.

"Never! I *own* this town!"

"No, you will now be a resident of the jail cell next to your pyro sister's," Tyler cut in.

Stacey screamed. "This wouldn't have happened if the damn love potion would have worked. He should have been mine! Instead, he turned into a freak!"

Tyler stuffed the disgraced siblings in the back of his cruiser and slammed the door. The crowd cheered, and Matt shook his head.

Stacey had drugged him all those years go.

That's why he was a ghost.

"Oh my God," Jordan whispered.

He pulled her into his arms, but she pulled away. "What baby?"

"It's my fault. All if it. Oh, God, Matt."

He tilted his head, utterly confused. "What is, baby?"

She looked up at him, her gaze emotionless. "That night I had made a vanishing potion. I wanted to stay hidden...to disappear."

He grew cold. "Why would you want to do that?"

"Because I hated the way people treated me. Stacey must have stolen it after I refused to make her a love potion. Damn, I should have noticed it was missing, but I just didn't care when I left. I left so quickly, I didn't even count up my potion bottles."

"And she laced my drink," Matt said, putting it together.

"So you disappeared, literally. And it's my fault. Fuck, Matt. I was so worried about me, I didn't protect you. What kind of woman does that make me?"

He gripped her arms, fear crawling up his

spine. "Human. It wasn't your fault. It was Stacey's. And Prescott's for being an ass."

She shook her head, her body frozen. "No, I have to go. I did all this. I need to go."

"No, you can't."

She tugged free and ran, the crowed parting for her, sorrow and pity in their gazes.

"Jordan!" He started toward her, but Justin held him back.

"Give her time, bro."

He tried to pull away, but Jackson held his other arm. "I need to go."

"We know," Jackson said. "We'll get her back to you. She just needs time. You know our Jordan."

Suddenly exhausted and overwhelmed be everything that had happened, Matt collapsed, his knees hitting the dirt. His brothers sat next to him silently. He watched as the firefighters worked on the old Marlow place.

It was gone.

Charred ruins and smoking embers. A memory of a time when he'd been someone else, and, just like the burning tomb in front of him, his heart felt as though it were fighting a losing battle.

He couldn't lose Jordan.

Not again.

Chapter 13

"I'm not going, Justin." Jordan packed the last of her suitcases and turned away from the man who refused to leave her alone.

Matt hadn't come.

She felt like a cliché, being one of those women who wanted the man to chase after her. That just made her want to leave even more. She didn't like the person she was becoming. She'd find a job outside of Holiday and leave her mistakes here.

"You have to come. We're doing a huge Cooper dinner at Jackson's, and you'll be missed."

"I doubt that."

"Okay, stop with this poor-me crap."

Surprised, she turned. "Excuse me?"

"You heard me. Yeah, I get it. Life sucks. But you know what? At least you're alive to know it sucks."

"I hurt him, Justin."

"No, Stacey did. Using something she *stole*. That doesn't make it your fault. That makes Stacey a sociopathic bitch."

"As much as I like hearing you say that, I still can't."

"You have to. Matt's hurting, Jor."

"And it's my fault."

"You can fix it by coming home. We'll take care of you. You're family."

She shook her head as her heart hurt. "You guys have always been amazing, but what happens when I go back into town? Things can't change that quickly."

"You'd be surprised. Now that Prescott and Stacey are facing hard time, the town feels lighter. They knew you were in there, Jor. They tried to kill you. As for the town, I think it was mostly the two of them scaring people into submission. Their family had so much money invested in every part of the town that people were afraid to go against them. But things are changing, Jordan."

"Justin, just let me go."

"Nope. I can't. You're coming to dinner, even if I have to drag you."

She narrowed her eyes. "You wouldn't."

"Oh, I would."

"Fine."

"Good, because you're being an idiot."

She knew she was. In fact, she didn't think she'd ever actually leave. It had taken her all night to pack when it should have only taken an hour. She wanted to stay but was too afraid to say it.

Justin drove her to Jackson's. He'd refused to let her drive herself because of her getaway vehicle. She rolled her eyes and winced. Her forehead still hurt from the fire, but she was getting better.

"He loves you, you know. We all do."

"I know, Justin. But it was all my fault."

"No, it was Stacey's. Get it through your skull, Matt doesn't blame you. We don't either.

You're our sister. You can't just leave us."

He reached out and gripped her hand and she smiled. She loved all the Cooper boys. God, she missed Matt. Why the hell had she been packing? She loved Matt and wanted to be part of Holiday. How could she leave?

Jordan wasn't going to leave. Not this time.

She couldn't run from her problems again.

She couldn't run from Matt.

They pulled up, and Matt ran to the car, pulled open the door, and kissed her hard. She wrapped her arms around his neck and moaned into his mouth.

God, she loved his mouth.

"Subtle, Matt. Subtle." Justin laughed as he walked inside, leaving her and Matt alone.

She pulled back and took a deep breath. "I love you."

"I love you too. Don't leave me like that again."

"I'm sorry."

"Don't be sorry, just don't do it again."

She smiled. "Okay."

"And before, when you made that potion? This town shouldn't have given you reasons to want to disappear. I'm sorry you felt that way, baby."

She shook her head. "It wasn't your fault. You were my only good thing back then."

He kissed her again, and she melted against him.

"Marry me," he whispered.

"What?" She could not have heard him right, though her heart sped up.

He laughed. "Marry me. Be my everything. You already are."

"Yes. A thousand times yes!" She squealed, and he picked her up and twirled her around the front lawn.

"Hey, kids, stop goofing off and get in here," Jackson ordered from the front porch. He tried to sound menacing, but Jordan could see the slight smile on his face he couldn't hide completely. "I made dinner, and you know how often that happens. So get your asses in here." With that, he stormed back in, and Matt laughed. Jackson always seemed to have a stormy outlook on life but Jordan didn't know why.

"Ahh, I think he likes me," Jordan teased.

"He loves you, just like the rest of my

brothers."

"Oh, really?" She quirked a brow.

"Not as much as me. And if any of them touch you, I'll kill them."

"Have I told you how much I like this whole caveman act on you? It's cute."

"Cute? I'm fierce."

She patted his chest. "Sure, baby."

Matt growled and led her to the door. "I'll get you back for that."

She brightened. "Really? With a table?"

He groaned. "Babe, we're about to go eat with my brothers at the dining room table. Don't put those images in my head."

"I can't help it. I like being bent over things," she whispered.

"You're a witch, you know that?"

She beamed. "And proud of it."

"It's about time you got here. I'm starving," Tyler complained with a smile.

She sat, and they dove into their steaks, baked potatoes, corn, and rolls. A real man's meal. She groaned at the perfectly cooked steak. Oh, hell, screw the man's meal; a woman couldn't have asked for a better meal.

Jordan looked up at Justin, who wasn't eating. He was looking rather pale and sick. He looked a bit distracted and off-center.

"What's wrong, Justin?" she asked.

He looked up, his gaze a bit off. "What? Oh, I'm just not feeling well, I guess. Don't worry about me."

She nodded but was determined to keep an eye on him. After all, he was going to be her brother. She felt at peace and warm at that thought.

As the rest dug in, Matt nudged her knee, an odd look on his face. "Did you hear the news?"

"What news?"

Jackson put his fork down and took a sip of his beer. "There was a vote today on who should replace Prescott."

She blinked. "Really? That was fast. Who won? No wait, let me guess? Jackson?"

The man in question let out a dry laugh. "Oh no, I'm not the lucky one."

"Then who?"

"You, baby," Matt said.

"Uh, what?" The men broke out in laughter, and she felt like she was missing the joke. "You can't be serious."

"Oh yes, baby. They wanted someone they trust in power."

"So they picked me? They don't trust me." Yeah, *so* not right.

"Yep," Matt answered. "It seems they wanted someone they knew would do a good job. They've seen you with the kids at school and know you care, Jordan. Plus, they know you have experience in PR. Plus, we're changing so many laws because we're losing the old ways, they want someone fresh. We have lawyers who can deal with the nitty-gritty details, but they want someone to be upfront and honest. They wanted to show you that they were on your side."

She sat there speechless.

They wanted her to be their mayor?

She felt like breaking out a rendition of Sally Field's *"They like me; they really like me!"* But that felt crass.

"So, Ms. Mayor, what do you say?" Justin asked, his face still pale.

"I say I have no idea what I'm doing, but hell yeah!"

Jackson held up his glass. "To Mayor Jordan Cross."

"Make that Mayor Jordan Cooper," Matt corrected.

"Holy shit!" Bray yelled. "Congrats!"

The rest of the brothers congratulated them, touching her arms and shoulders and patting Matt on the back. She settled against him and smiled. This was her family. Her home. Why had she ever wanted to leave it?

"I love you, Jordan. You're mine."

"Just like you're mine. I love you too."

"You know, you utterly charmed me."

"Anytime, ghost boy, any time."

The End

Coming soon in the Holiday, Montana World, Santa's Executive.

Justin's Story.

Take a look at Carrie Ann Ryan's other work like,
Dust of My Wings

Chapter 1

A summons from the council never led to good things. Shade Griffin's millennia worth of experience told him that. No matter what he truly desired, he'd do what he was told. He didn't have another option, and why would he disobey now? He never had before. Whatever demands they dealt might seem tedious to a long-lived being such as him, he didn't have anything else better to do.

Such was the life of an angel in his predicament; a vast and endless sense of being, yet no one with whom to share it.

Shade shook off the misery that threatened to creep along his skin and suffocate him. The idea of sharing his endless life with someone else, someone special, had long since burned away. No need to think about it again.

The sun broke through the clouds, warming his cool, honey-colored, almost dark tan, skin. He lifted his face, letting the rays soak into his pores. His eyes closed, and he took a deep breath, not really wanting to leave the spot. He rolled his neck, stretching his muscles, and then opened his eyes. His back ached from the long flight to the enclave. He stretched his wings, the light shimmering off his midnight black wings that trailed to a rim of deep blue. The wind picked up, his blue-black hair flowing behind him.

Shade arched his back, his wings flared, and blue dust trickled off and into the air, and drifted to the ground below.

Damn stuff kept doing that; and there was nothing he could do about it. He clenched his fists and winced in pain. He looked down at the healing abrasions on his knuckles and muttered a curse.

As one of the appointed enforcers of angelic law, he'd just come back from the punishment of a young angel: a cocky one at that. He hated doing it, but the unrepentant jerk had decided it would be fun to fly in broad daylight without cloud cover over Area 51. Really? Cliché much? It was easy enough to downplay the event as another UFO sighting, which would certainly bring out the crazies, but it didn't negate the fact that the reckless angel had broken angelic law by letting humans see him flying.

Because he had decided to laugh about it to his friends and merely shrugged it off, Shade had to step in. If he'd apologized, then Shade wouldn't have had to use his fists. But no. The young one mouthed off and challenged him, so Shade had to accept. After all, as a warrior, he could not ignore a challenge. Doing so would negate his authority.

And he won.

Of course.

He still hated punishing others, even though it was his job. Between him and his best friend, Ambrose, who was practically his brother, they dealt with most of the enforcing the angelic laws. Together they'd done what they had to do for centuries, and in Ambrose's case, even longer.

Shade was a warrior angel. In the times of the Angelic Wars, he'd fought alongside the best of the best. Hell, he was the best of the best. Well, maybe tied with Ambrose, but he wouldn't tell the other angel that.

Shade chuckled as he envisioned Ambrose's reaction to his thought. Ambrose was sure to want to prove just the opposite to be the case, and Shade would be more than willing to give it a go. *If you couldn't fight for supremacy with your best friend, how else would you even know how good you were?*

Now those wars were long since over. Times of awkward peace were at hand, meaning the warriors herded the other angels and made sure they followed the rules the council members set in place.

They followed the rules, even if the rules were sometimes, in his opinion, too strict for their own good. But he would never voice it. He was merely a warrior angel.

He wasn't even a godly one like in the fables of mortals. Their race wasn't that of a god. Yes, if theology was correct, a god at some point had created them, but they weren't God's right hand men; they were not the symbol of goodness and hope. Far from it. They were just another species with rules, regulations, and a seemingly endless long life in order to be subjugated.

Wow. Bitter much?

He shouldn't be; he had everything he wanted, didn't he? His forehead scrunched as he thought, and his wings fluttered a bit in agitation.

He certainly had all the money, titles, glory, and privileges a warrior of the finest caliber could have. Why did he feel like he was missing something?

Shade shook his head and looked around. He stood at a midpoint on the mountainside, the enclave circling him. Stone buildings jutted from rock faces, thousands of feet above the surface, old as time. No stairs or elevators here. Open the door and, without wings, they'd drop to their death. Marble and crystal twinkled in the sunlight from the adornments and windows on all of the structures. It may have looked cold to some, but to Shade and his angelic brethren it was warm and inviting.

It looked like home, but it wasn't truly a 'home'; There was no love waiting on the other side of the door, and that pained him.

He sighed. He really needed to stop thinking such depressing thoughts. Taking one last look at the place he called home, he jumped off the ledge, his wings spreading to catch a drift, as the cool breezes hit his skin. He flew past other angels in the air, nodding to a few, but kept to himself. He was a warrior angel, the last face some would see as they stared beyond the end of his blade. Tough to make life-long friends outside of certain circles that way.

Shade descended, the wind whipping his hair back from his face, until his feet touched the stone balcony set off the council chambers. He set his wings back, making sure they didn't trail on the floor. He was exhausted, but that didn't give him a reason to be lazy. He walked through the ornate doors that reached tall to the roof. Despite his thousand years of living, sometimes the immense beauty of the council chambers had him at a loss for words.

Gold and crystal adorned the walls. Intricate carvings and art filled the room. Eons of pride and talent gave the room a sense of grandeur and honor that made Shade feel young in relation to the other angels surrounding him.

In reality, he was the youngest warrior angel of them all, and second in command to Ambrose, the leader of the warriors, the best at the job. That wasn't pride talking, just fact.

Shade walked to the center of the room and surveyed the five council members before him, perched high on their thrones, their noses turned up towards him. Another presence worried him. Ambrose stood off to the side, a frown on his face. What was happening?

"I see you have finally decided to grace us with your presence," Caine, the leader and all-around pain-in-the ass, admonished, and Shade held in a scowl. The brown-haired angel lifted a lip as if the mere sight of him disgusted the ruler.

Shade bowed his head. "I'm sorry I was late. I had just finished my dealing with the young angel and needed time to clear my head before I came. I didn't want to taint the council with the thoughts and actions of a warrior." There. That didn't sound like sarcasm and distain, did it? Well, maybe it did, but it was the best he could do. He wasn't overly happy with Ambrose in the council chamber. It felt like an ambush.

Caine snorted and shook his head.

Okay, apparently he couldn't quite mask his true feelings. Oh, well.

Shade didn't hate the council. He just didn't like the fact that they held all the power and didn't seem to do anything but hand out decrees and punishments that were enforced by the warriors. There were only three classes of angles: the council, the warriors, and the others. He didn't like all the power on the top that trickled down to nothing, but who was he to speak out of turn?

"Enough of your pleasantries. We need you here, now," Striker, the second-in-command, cut in. Dishwater brown hair and plain features made him look almost human. If it weren't for the brown wings coming out of his back, he'd look like a mortal. Maybe that's why the angel was always an ass.

"Okay." Shade nodded. "What is it that you need?" He once again wondered why Ambrose was there? Why did they need two warrior angels? Tingles of dread filled his belly. Had the other faction of angels done something? They hadn't destroyed the rebels completely in the war. It was always a cause for trepidation and concern that the others would come back and start something. Were they on the brink of another war? He'd not heard anything, but he couldn't be too sure.

"We have been alerted to a breach of security," Caine announced. "Our secrets may be unraveled soon if this is not fixed."

"You mean the secrets of the supernatural?" Shade asked. "How can that be?"

Striker gave a laugh, filled with bile rather than humor. "You dare ask this when it is your fault we are in this predicament in the first place?"

Shade froze. "What?"

"Your dust." Striker sneered. "Your oh-so-favorable blue dust has been collected by a human. If it falls into the wrong hands, do you understand what will happen? Everything that has been held secret for eons will be lost because you have a dusting problem."

Oh, crap.

As a child, he'd had a problem with his dust. Whenever he got excited or angry, he'd sprinkle dust where he flew or stood. Beyond a few occurrences recently, he'd thought he'd conquered it years ago. How had someone gotten it? Did they even know what it was?

"I didn't know," Shade whispered.

But that was a lie. He did know. Just that morning, he'd seen a sprinkle of his dust flowing on the wind and thought nothing of it.

My God. What have I done?

"We know you didn't," said Agnes, the sole female member of the council. Her piercing blue eyes filled with understanding.

Of all the council members, Shade liked her best.

"But," Agnes continued, "you must fix it, Shade. Finish it. Find your dust and reclaim it before someone finds out what it is. We don't have the power to wipe the memories of an incidence such as this from a human's mind as we once did. The humans don't believe anymore. Because they don't, we've lost our ability to shield ourselves the way we should."

Shade nodded, sadness and frustration setting root.

"I will fix this," Shade promised. "You have my word."

The council nodded and dismissed him. With a glance toward Ambrose, Shade left the room, his best friend on his heels.

The two friends didn't speak once they reached the end of the balcony. They simply jumped off the edge, their wings catching the wind, and flew toward another mountaintop. Shade needed time to think. To calculate.

He was damned fine at his job. Strong and fierce. Yet a childhood problem of dusting could take down a civilization. He would have laughed at the ridiculousness of that statement if it hadn't been true.

They landed, their feet settling on the soil. Shade looked behind him at the place he called home. They didn't live in heaven because they weren't godly angels, far from it. He wasn't even sure there was a heaven beyond their time. Their world was in the same realm as the humans, but it was tucked away in a pocket of space between two mountain ranges, hidden from the eyes of the unknown.

A few raindrops fell from the sky before turning to a slight mist. The other angels who were at a lower altitude flew to the safety of their homes, the rain beginning to weigh heavy on their wings. Only the strongest could fly in anything more than mist, another reason they didn't live on clouds, as most humans seemed to believe. One flight through a dense cloud could be dangerous; the moisture seeped into their feathers and threatened to drag the angel down. Without sufficient muscular back strength, the angel would plummet.

Most didn't. Despite the vast strength they possessed, angels were weak in some respects.

"Are you going to stand there in the rain and watch others while everything falls around you, or are you going to fix this?" Ambrose's deep voice cut through his thoughts, and Shade turned toward him.

Tall with white blond hair pulled back from his pale face in a braid, with white, almost crystal wings, Ambrose was the light to Shade's dark. Yet, the colors masked the personality, for where Shade saw the humor and light in some things, his best friend was the dark, the edge to the blade. Shade, too, held his own fury; he just didn't show it as often.

Dangerous and agile, his mentor had taught him everything he knew. Shade lowered his head in shame. He'd failed.

"You didn't fail, Shade," Ambrose whispered.

"I didn't say that aloud." Ambrose was always doing that. He was practically a mind reader

"You didn't have to. We all leave trails of angel dust. You are no different from others except that you leave greater quantities. It's not something to be shameful of."

"I beg to differ."

"It's only different this time because it got into the hands of a human. I'm worried how it got there, which is why I was in the room when you came in."

Intrigued, Shade lifted his head. "What are you saying?"

Ambrose shrugged. "I don't know yet. Something just seems off to me, but I will work on finding out."

"Okay, what else do you know?"

"Only that the dust may be in the hands of a woman."

"A woman?" Interesting.

The motorcycle vibrated beneath Shade as he pulled off the side of the road and parked. The rain pelted him, the cold seeping into his bones, but he shrugged it off. He was in northern Washington, and this seemed to be the norm in terms of weather.

He lifted his leg and got off the bike, ignoring the stares of the women around him. They watched him stroll, his powerful legs leading to long strides. He'd tucked his wings into the slits in his back to hide the fact he was an angel, but he couldn't hide his face or the fact that women seemed to fawn over it.

It had been a long time since he had a woman, not since that jaguar shifter a century or two before on a night of deep depression and loneliness. But the heat, claws, and desperation had served to fill only a physical need that left him even lonelier than before. From that moment on, he left his carnal needs up to his hand. Before the jaguar, it had been even longer, but he didn't want to think about her. The one he'd lost. She was long since gone.

Shade walked into a nearby café, the smells of baked goods and coffee filling his nose. He ordered a small coffee then went back to sit at a table near the window so he could watch those who passed by. A male pixie, in human form, walked in front of the window and nodded toward him. There were so many supernatural beings hidden from view in the world that Shade couldn't even count them.

All humans were diluted forms of supernaturals. For millennia, the supernaturals had bred with one another and mixed the species until, finally, their powers had dwindled in most, and they stopped believing in things that came out of fairy tales. Those with so little non-human blood running their veins that they seemed ordinary were now called humans, although each had at least something beyond human lying dormant in their DNA.

Council did not identify the name of the human who collected the dust, but Ambrose told Shade it was about to be in the hands of a woman who lived and worked nearby. Her name was Lily.

Who was this Lily? Shade wanted to get a look at her. She had the answers. She possessed the reason behind his shame: his blue dust.

A woman with expressive emerald-green eyes passed by the window; a slight smile graced her face, and she had those side-swoopy bangs women loved so much. She was of average height and held delicious curves. He looked over every inch of her—a small waist, large, perfect breasts to fit his palms, slightly wide hips that would serve well when he gripped them, and sexy legs beneath the hem of her brown coat...

Lily.

That had to be her. He didn't know how he knew, but he was sure of it.

His groin tightened.

She was human. Not a lick of anything else came from her. Yet, why did he want her so from just a look? He'd never looked at a human this way before. Why now? Was it because she might be the one who held his dust?

Lily stopped under the awning right in front of the window, careful of where she stepped—*odd*—and brushed the hair out of her eyes, before smiling at a passerby. She was radiant. Absolutely gorgeous. Shade held back a groan and shifted uncomfortably in his seat when she bit into her lip. She smiled again then walked to what must have been her car, got in, and left before Shade even thought to stand.

Some warrior he was, completely frozen in shock by his reaction to her. He was, however, unrepentant. He didn't want to follow her today anyway. A town small as this would know of Lily and aide him in his research. If the supernaturals were revealed, chaos would rain. Humans could feel threatened, start wars, do untold atrocities when they met with what they didn't know and therefore feared. If the supernaturals felt threatened...Shade didn't want to think about that. He had to know more before he did anything.

So many questions flashed through his mind. Who was she? Why did she have his dust? What would she do if she discovered his secret?

Most importantly, he wondered if she was

single and how she would look underneath him, blushing in ecstasy.

Shade shook his head, dispelling those annoying thoughts. He'd find out what he needed to about Lily, get his dust, and save the entirety of the supernatural world. Maybe along the way he'd learn a little more about a pretty brunette whose very presence threatened to make his wings stretch to the sky.

Yep. Easy for a warrior angel such as himself.

ABOUT THE AUTHOR

Carrie Ann Ryan is a bestselling paranormal and contemporary romance author. After spending too much time behind a lab bench, she decided to dive into the romance world and find her werewolf mate - even if its just in her books. Happy endings are always near - even if you have to get over the challenges of falling in love first.

Her first book, *An Alpha's Path*, is the first in her Redwood Pack series. She's also an avid reader and lover of romance and fiction novels. She loves meeting new authors and new worlds. Any recommendations you have are appreciated. Carrie Ann lives in New England with her husband and two kittens.

www.carrieannryan.com

18611938R00132

Made in the USA
Charleston, SC
12 April 2013